MYSTERIES *of* MARTHA'S VINEYARD

---

MYSTERIES *of* MARTHA'S VINEYARD

# Don't Rock
## *the*
# Boat

ELIZABETH LUDWIG

New York

# Don't Rock

*the*

# Boat

**To Ane and Michelle:**

Thank you for being such an encouragement to me! I love you both so much. This journey wouldn't be the same without you.

## CHAPTER ONE

Priscilla Latham Grant tugged her collar tightly around her ears and let the icy December wind whipping off the Atlantic sweep across her cheeks. She smiled as she inhaled deeply of the salt-scented air, so different than anything she'd experienced back in Kansas. There was something so invigorating about these early morning walks, something so encouraging and joyful. Even with scattered cloud cover, it promised to be a glorious day.

Giving the zipper on her warm winter coat one last snug under her chin, she set off for the staircase that led down to the beach. The sand gave beneath her feet with every step, making her daily walk more vigorous than normal, but she enjoyed the feeling of straining toward something. Today, the goal was a secluded cove just around the bend from her lighthouse.

Ahead of her, Jake romped in the light dusting of snow that capped the sand dunes. She barely heard his happy bark over the wind and pounding of the surf, but she knew he wouldn't stray far. He stopped every few feet and looked back at her, as though to say, *Come on, let's play.*

When he tired of that, he dashed into the frigid waves, chasing a fish or perhaps a scrap of seaweed. Priscilla groaned and curled her fingers inside her mittens. He would need a bath after this walk was over.

She rose to her tiptoes. "Jake, come back."

He ignored her and zipped into a mound of swaying beach grass. She cupped one hand to her mouth and called again over the crashing waves. "Jake!"

His twitching tail said he heard but wasn't inclined to obey. He lifted his head and then stiffened, his tail going ramrod straight.

Priscilla frowned. He was below her, near the shore. She picked her way down the slight hill toward him, mindful that the sand could easily give way and send her tumbling. "Jake, what are you looking at?"

He barked once and then began an incessant yapping that grew louder as she picked up her pace. Her calves complained as her booted feet dug into the sand. Granted, she took these walks for exercise, but her muscles were going to complain tomorrow.

"What is it, boy?" Priscilla struggled for breath against the sharp bite of the wind. "What do you see?"

Jake's furry head turned toward her, and his warm chocolate eyes begged her to come and look. She reached for his collar and tugged him back from something half-buried in the sand. "What is that?"

He whimpered and began clawing frantically, throwing bits of grass and sand all over himself and Priscilla.

"Stop, Jake," she commanded. She nudged him aside with her foot and bent for a closer look. Hints of brown peeked through the clumps of seaweed and sand. She also thought she glimpsed the sheen of metal. A clasp of some sort?

Curling her lip in disgust, she reached down and pulled the seaweed back, exposing bits of tattered leather. "A briefcase?"

She looked at Jake, who tipped his head to stare at her curiously. If he could talk, he surely would have asked, *What's a briefcase?*

Priscilla dropped to her knees in the cold sand. With fingers curled inside her mittens, she scraped back enough of the sand to see that the object was much larger than a briefcase.

"It's a suitcase."

She turned, but Jake had lost interest in the discovery and was nipping at the seaweed she'd pushed aside. Now he'd smell of wet sand *and* fish. She'd be lucky to get the smell out of his fur with two baths.

Bending back to her task, Priscilla continued digging until she had most of the suitcase exposed. A couple of tugs on the handle, and it slid free. Despite the scratches marring the surface, she could tell the suitcase was good quality. Leather straps with brass buckles protected each end, and there was a brass lock below the handle for added security. Priscilla eyed it curiously. How had a suitcase ended up on her beach?

A foghorn sounded, and Priscilla looked up to see a gleaming ship chugging toward shore. Judging by its size, it would probably end up in Boston Harbor. She glanced back at the suitcase. Plenty of ships sailed past her beach and the Misty Harbor Lighthouse left to her by her aunt, Marjorie Latham, and that wasn't even counting the ones that ferried tourists from the mainland every day. This old suitcase could have come from any one of them. Or worse…a boat could have capsized.

Concern gripped her as she looked both ways up the beach. She hated to think of a person struggling in the frigid waters of the Atlantic. This time of year, it wouldn't take long to succumb to hypothermia, and that was assuming they could fight their way through the pounding waves.

Fortunately, only rippling sand and swaying grass stretched along the shore. Priscilla breathed a relieved sigh and then tipped the suitcase upright and gave it a shake. It didn't feel empty. She stood and picked it up by the handle. It was heavy, but that could simply be because it was waterlogged. The only way to know for sure was to drag it back to the cottage and pry open the lock.

"Jake!"

This time when she called, he bounded to her side, his fur wet and matted with sand.

"You know you're not coming into the house like that, right?" she scolded.

Oblivious to his bedraggled condition, Jake yipped happily and ran on ahead. Tipping the suitcase onto one edge, Priscilla half-dragged, half-carried it up the beach toward her cottage. Too bad it didn't have wheels like its more modern counterpart—not that wheels would have helped much in the sand, she realized, as she bumped it up the stairs onto her porch. Pausing to catch her breath, she swiped the back of her hand over her brow and rested her hip against the side of the cottage. Walks on the beach were one thing, but what she'd just done amounted to a full-fledged workout.

She took off her mittens and studied her raw hands. Blisters were already forming on her palms. Maybe later she could swing by

Candy Lane's bakery and indulge in a couple of her favorite chocolate chip cookies as a reward for having worked so hard. But first…

She bent and clasped the suitcase handle, bumping and dragging it inside until it rested fully on her kitchen table. She grimaced at the trail of sand left in her wake. She'd only dragged in half the beach with her. Jake gave himself a shake and deposited the other half on the floor.

"Jake, no!"

She sighed as he trotted off toward the living room. She'd have to sweep up the mess later. Right now she was dying for a peek inside that suitcase.

She paused. Maybe she should examine it first and see if she could figure out to whom it belonged before breaking open the lock. Though she longed to give in to her curiosity, practicality won out. She slid out of her coat, then grabbed a damp cloth and began wiping away the sand and grit that remained while she looked for initials or a luggage tag. When she didn't find any, she bit her lip and bent to examine the lock.

A warm, furry body bumped against her legs. Jake had returned, his ears perked and his head tilted to one side as he looked at her.

"What?" Priscilla shooed him with the towel. "It's your fault we even have this suitcase. After all, you're the one who found it."

Jake settled to the floor with a moan, his head resting glumly on his paws.

She smiled. Having Jake around was like having a live-in friend. She talked to him like a real person, and sometimes she was certain he understood.

Leaning down, Priscilla investigated the lock. It was the old-fashioned variety—the kind that needed a key to open. She gave it a jiggle, and a few grains of wet sand spattered onto the table.

"Great. More sand." She gave the suitcase another jiggle. "Well, Jake, I certainly won't be able to get this lock open until I get all the sand out."

Sighing, she crossed to the cupboards, pulled out a drawer, and rummaged until she found a basting brush. "Perfect."

She scooped up the brush and set about removing as much of the sand as she could from the lock. When that was done, she went back to the drawer and removed a small paring knife. Though it was slim, the blade was still too thick to fit in the lock. She set the knife aside and frowned. Now what?

Her gaze settled on a grill fork. She lifted an eyebrow. Before he died, her husband Gary had teased her a time or two about her makeshift tools—butter knives instead of screwdrivers, and heeled shoes instead of hammers—but this was one instance where she was glad for her unique way of viewing the items in her cupboards and closets.

She carried the two-tined fork to the suitcase. After a little finagling, she realized the long, slender tines would fit in the lock, but she would have to bend one of them out of the way if she wanted to slide the other inside.

She went back to the cupboard, but this time she came back with a pair of pliers she kept handy and made short work of the second tine on the grill fork. As she'd thought, the remaining tine slid easily into the lock, and with only a little coaxing from the flat side of the pliers, she was able to force it open.

At the satisfying click, Jake lifted his head and peered up at her. Priscilla rested her hand against the top of the suitcase and met his gaze. "Well? Are we sure we want to know what's inside?"

He gave a soft whimper.

"I'm curious too, but what if we don't like what we find?"

Jake yawned, as if to say, *What could possibly be so bad?*

"Right." She sucked in a breath. "Here goes nothing."

Though she wanted to look, Priscilla's heart beat a peculiar rhythm as she reached for the handle. This suitcase had belonged to someone once. What if that person lost their life in the Atlantic? Would they really want her riffling through their things? She shuddered at the morbid thought. On the other hand, how would she ever know whose it was if she didn't look inside? Obviously, she wouldn't.

The argument settled, she took a deep breath, counted to three, and then slowly lifted the lid.

## CHAPTER TWO

Now that the suitcase was open, Jake's interest in his beach treasure revived. He sat up and pawed at Priscilla's leg, giving a low whimper.

"Shush, Jake." She patted the dog's head, but her attention remained fixed on the contents of the suitcase, all of which were disheveled and slightly waterlogged, and which oddly included very few clothes.

"What is this?"

She frowned as she picked up a large flashlight and shook it. Brown, rusty water dripped from the end onto her table and splattered onto her sweater.

"Ugh. So much for the batteries. They're probably completely corroded."

The flashlight was heavy and black, and it reminded her of the ones she'd seen clipped to the belts on police officers. She clicked the power button and wasn't at all surprised when it failed to light up. She set it aside on the table and pulled out a pair of binoculars. They were coated with sand but not broken. She gave them a cursory investigation and then set them next to the flashlight.

Jake whined. Priscilla sighed in exasperation as he nudged her with his nose. "What is it, boy?"

He rose on his back feet, balancing like a circus dog as he sniffed at the suitcase.

"Get down." Priscilla gave his chest a small shove, but he refused to budge. "I know you found the suitcase, but it's not yours," she scolded. Grabbing his collar, she led him to the kitchen door and urged him out into the backyard. Normally he loved playing outside, but today he whirled and pressed his nose to the jamb as she carefully eased the door shut.

"You would think you were part basset hound, the way you're carrying on," she muttered to him through the door. "Note to self—buy more chew toys for Jake the next time you're in town."

Smiling, she rubbed the sand from her hands and crossed back to the table. Maybe now she could finish sifting through the suitcase in peace. But before she could dig in, her cell phone rang. Seeing the name on the display, Priscilla grabbed the phone and pushed the Answer button eagerly.

"Gerald, I'm so glad you called."

She *was* glad, but she wasn't surprised. From the moment she'd moved from Kansas to Martha's Vineyard, the handsome Coast Guard captain always seemed to turn up precisely when she needed him.

"Priscilla? Is everything all right?"

"Everything's fine." Realizing she'd answered rather brusquely, she forced herself to slow down. "I'm sorry, Gerald. Yes, everything is fine." She tapped the side of her phone with her finger. "Listen, do you have a moment to stop by this morning? I have something I would like to show you."

She paced as she talked, and her gaze darted to the suitcase and the trail of sand that still littered her floor.

"Of course," he exclaimed. "That's actually why I was calling. I was hoping you might have time for a cup of coffee."

Her face heated with embarrassment. In all the excitement, she'd not even given him a chance to explain his reason for calling. "Oh, Gerald, I'm so sorry. That was a very poor display of manners."

He chuckled easily, his voice a husky tremor in her ear. "Whatever you have to show me must really be something to have you so riled up."

"I think so." She smiled. "I'll start a pot of coffee."

"Sounds good. I'll stop by Candy's and grab a couple of her cranberry muffins and then head on over."

"And some chocolate chip cookies?"

He laughed. "And some cookies. See you in a few minutes."

Priscilla hung up, brought Jake inside and locked him in his kennel, then hurried to sweep up the kitchen floor. When she finished, she crossed to the sink to fill the coffeepot. Gerald's life was well ordered and punctual, and if he said it would be a few minutes, that was exactly how long it would be. In fact, the coffee was still brewing when she heard a knock on the front door. She hurried to answer, her breath catching in her throat as she caught sight of his tall frame and broad shoulders through the glass.

Priscilla's hand rose to her hair. The walk on the beach had been windy, and after digging through the suitcase, she was also covered in sand and more than likely smelled like kelp. Wishing she'd taken a moment to check her appearance, she pasted on a smile and opened the door. "Hi, Gerald. Thanks for coming over."

He smiled, his hazel eyes twinkling as he held up a bag stamped with the Candy Lane Confectionery logo. "No problem. I'll take any excuse for one of Candy's muffins."

Instantly, she felt at ease. Gerald had never seemed like someone who stood much on propriety. She laughed and opened the door wider. "Me too. Come on in."

He entered, turning his shoulders to fit past her in the narrow hall. When he was inside, she closed the door and then stood admiring the way he filled up the space, exactly the way a man should, in her opinion.

Gerald's eyebrows rose. "So you have something to show me?"

"Yes." She blinked and motioned toward his Coast Guard parka. "May I take your coat?"

While he shrugged out of it, Priscilla gave herself a mental shake. Heavens, she really had to get a handle on her thoughts. The Good Book said that was where problems started, and it had been her experience to trust what she read.

She hung his coat on the hooks next to the door and then pointed toward the kitchen. "It's back here. Jake found a suitcase on the beach this morning."

"He found a what?"

Priscilla nodded and led him down the hall. "I know. I thought it was a briefcase at first, but when I started digging, I realized it was much larger. *Much* larger. And wet. It took me twenty minutes to drag it up from the beach."

She went on to explain how she'd carefully examined it before breaking it open to look inside.

Interest gleamed in Gerald's eyes as they entered the kitchen. Catching sight of the suitcase, he crossed to the table and tilted the lid up slightly to look at the front and sides. "It looks old. Where did you say you found it?"

"On the beach, just past the lighthouse. Actually, Jake found it. We were headed toward the cove."

While he looked at the suitcase, Priscilla spotted more sand on the floor. She swept it under the table with her foot.

"Huh."

She looked up quickly. "Hmm?"

Gerald picked up the flashlight to examine it more closely. "This is a pretty impressive tac light." He set it down next to the binoculars. "What else is in there?"

She shrugged. "I don't know. You called before I could check." She moved to stand beside him and reached into the suitcase. With two fingers, she plucked out a soggy envelope and carefully peeled back the flap to look inside. "It's money. At least, I think it is."

She showed him and then pulled out several strange-looking bills and laid them out on the table.

Gerald frowned as he watched. "Whoever owned this suitcase must have traveled a lot to carry so many types of foreign currency. And what is that?" He pointed to another soggy piece of paper. "Is that a map of the Vineyard?"

He reached into the suitcase. Priscilla watched curiously as he clasped a rumpled piece of paper by the edge and carefully unfolded it. It did appear to be a map of the island. Several spots along the coast were differentiated with smudged *X*'s. One mark in particular caught her eye. Priscilla caught her breath. The inky lines trickled all over Misty Harbor and her lighthouse.

"M-maybe the suitcase belonged to a tourist," she said quietly. "All those *X*'s could be spots they wanted to see before they left the island."

"Maybe." Gerald didn't sound convinced. The lines crisscrossing his forehead deepened as he thought. "What else have we got?"

They dug carefully through the remaining items—a couple of men's shirts, several hats, a pair of fancy sunglasses in a case, and a rather strange-looking knife. But it was several small photos tucked deep into a side pocket of the suitcase that interested Priscilla the most. Somehow, they had managed to stay dry when everything else was wet. She held one of them up for Gerald to see.

"Look at this. Maybe this will give us a clue to the owner of the suitcase."

He set down the knife and examined the photo. "It's kind of a strange picture. It's just the man's face and he's looking straight into the camera, but he's not smiling."

Priscilla studied the man's face over Gerald's shoulder. He was handsome and appeared to be in his late thirties or early forties, clean-shaven, but with an earnest stare that made her think he was much older. "This photograph sort of reminds me of those old-timey pictures people used to take before all the high-tech equipment. They had to hold really still in order to get a good print."

He nodded. "I know what you're talking about. It's called a tintype. But this one is modern. Look at his shirt."

Priscilla leaned in close and frowned. "You're right. It's a button-down."

"What about the other pictures?"

She showed them to him. They were very similar to the first photo, except one depicted a woman and the other a much older man with a full, gray beard.

"They must be the owners of the suitcase, don't you think?" she asked.

Gerald scratched his chin. "Not necessarily. The owner could have been carrying those pictures for any number of reasons, though they don't exactly look like family photos."

"More like mug shots."

"Exactly."

He handed the picture back to Priscilla, then reclaimed the knife. "This thing is pretty neat. It's old…like maybe World War II era. You don't see too many of these anymore. I wonder why anyone would carry it around in a suitcase?"

"Is it valuable?"

He balanced the handle across his palm. "To a collector, maybe."

"Do you think you could find out?"

"I could ask around."

While he examined the knife further, Priscilla studied the man in the photo—taking special note of the intensity of his gaze and the hard set of his jaw—before tucking the photo back into the suitcase.

"Oh, Gerald, this is just terrible. We have to find out who this suitcase belongs to and how it managed to wash up onto my beach. I'll always wonder if the owner drowned otherwise."

Gerald shook his head. "I don't think that's very likely. We haven't received any distress calls in the last few days, and there are no reports of missing boats."

His words eased the weight pressing heavily on her chest but couldn't dispel it. That wouldn't happen until she had an explanation for the mysterious suitcase and its owner. "I'm glad to hear that, but what about sightings from other watercraft? Has anyone reported seeing a boat in trouble? It could be that someone pitched the suitcase overboard. People do that when they're in danger of sinking, don't they?"

His shrug did not look certain, but he nodded. "It's possible. I'll check when I get back to the station."

The tension eased from Priscilla's shoulders. She washed the dirt from her hands in the sink and then crossed to the counter. "I appreciate your help, Gerald. Now, let's have that cup of coffee."

He fixed a longing glance on the bakery bag and then at his watch. "You know, if I head back to the station now, I should have just enough time to look through my reports for any sightings of distressed boats before I meet with the staff."

She smiled and took two cups from the cupboard. "And miss out on the snacks you brought from Candy's place?"

He took a whiff and then grinned and patted his stomach. "I was hoping you'd say that. The coffee smells good, and I saved space for those cookies."

While he washed up, Priscilla poured them each a cup—and tried very hard not to think about how it felt to have a man scrubbing up in her kitchen. She carried the coffee cups to the table, but with the contents of the suitcase spread everywhere, there wasn't room to set them down. She frowned. "Maybe we should go sit in the living room."

Gerald scooped up the bag from Candy's and followed her to the cozy living room overlooking the water. Along with a gently worn couch, there was a rocking chair by the window and an overstuffed wingback chair and matching ottoman that Priscilla liked to curl into on snowy evenings. When they sat, he handed her a napkin from the bag and one of the cookies, then took another for himself.

"Wow," he said around a mouthful of cookie and chocolate chips. "I can see why you love these things."

"Uh-huh." Priscilla laughed and set his cup on the coffee table. "What happened to your cranberry muffin?"

"I'm saving it for dessert." He took another bite of his cookie and sighed. "It's a good thing I limit my visits to Candy's."

Priscilla sipped her coffee and then reached for her cookie. "I go there more than I should, which is why I took up walking along the beach. It helps me work off those extra calories." She held up the cookie. "These things look innocent enough, but I've already gained four pounds since moving here."

He laughed. "You're smart, taking advantage of the beach while you can. This mild weather probably won't last much longer, not according to the charts down at the station."

Priscilla set down her cup and leaned forward on the couch. "Hopefully it'll last at least a few days longer. Christmas in Edgartown starts next week, and I've really been looking forward to it."

"I'm glad you're planning on going," Gerald said. "There'll be plenty to do, even if the weather isn't perfect. It's a lot of fun, and it'll give you a real taste for Christmas on the Vineyard."

"I'm sure it will be very different from the Christmases I spent in Kansas."

Thinking of home and her second Christmas without her husband, Gary, brought a touch of nostalgia to her heart. Thankfully, Gerald didn't leave her much time to ponder.

He grabbed a napkin and wiped the crumbs from his fingers. "Will your daughter be joining you for the holidays?"

"She's planning on it." She snapped her fingers and set down her cookie. "Which reminds me, I'll need to head to the mainland before the weather gets too bad to do a little last-minute shopping."

"Last-minute?" He laughed and dropped the napkin into the empty bag. "I haven't even *started* my Christmas shopping. Well, except for a few things I picked up here and there for…you know…friends."

His gaze dropped, and his cheeks filled with ruddy color, vibrant against his official navy blue Coast Guard sweater.

Priscilla's heart thumped. She had thought of him over the course of the last few weeks, and had even bought an antique sextant in Tisbury she thought he would like, as a thanks for all the help he'd given her over the last few months, but knowing he might also have shopped for her was different somehow. She cleared her throat and changed the subject.

"Normally, I have my Christmas shopping all done by this time. It's a habit I picked up early in my marriage, when times were lean. But this year…" She blew out a breath and reached for her cup. "Rachel is so hard to buy for, and I haven't found anything I think she'll really like. I've been debating about going into Boston to see if I can find something there that I think will catch her eye."

He shrugged. "Don't give up hope of finding something on the island. Edgartown goes all out for their festival. I'm sure you'll find something fun or unusual there."

"Thanks. I'll keep that in mind." She sipped her cooling coffee. "So what about you? Do you have plans for Christmas?"

He leaned back in his chair. "I had planned to take a few days off, but with Aggie due next month, I may have to push that back. It's been a difficult pregnancy, and I'd like to be there for her when my grandchild is born."

Concern tugged Priscilla's heart. "I hope everything is okay."

She read peace in his eyes—peace that could only come from faith in Someone greater than the physicians providing Aggie and her baby's care.

He smiled. "It should be. She's been going to Boston for regular checkups and receiving really good care, from what I hear."

Priscilla sighed happily. "A new grandbaby. How sweet. I can't wait until Rachel settles down and starts a family of her own." She eyed him over the rim of her cup. "I'm sorry that you won't get to take more time off at Christmas, though."

"It'll be okay. I'll have Christmas Eve and most of Christmas Day off. Aggie and the family are spending it with Nick's parents, but I'm sure I'll find something to keep me busy."

Though he said them without a trace of melancholy, the words instantly stirred compassion in Priscilla's heart. No one should be alone at Christmas, especially not someone as good and kind as Gerald.

"You're always welcome to spend it with us." The words popped from her mouth before she could consider them. She set her cup down hastily. "I mean, Gail, Trudy, and Joan and their families are coming by on Christmas Eve, so what's one more?" That still didn't come out the way she wanted. She bit her lip in frustration. "What I'm trying to say is, my cousins and I would love to have you."

His grin widened as she fumbled for words, and Priscilla found she couldn't help but smile with him.

"Well now, that was awkward," she said, laughing.

"I'm glad I'm not the only one," he said. "I'm never so much at a loss for words than when I'm around you."

As soon he said it, Gerald seemed to regret it. He clamped his mouth shut and rose to stand. "Anyway, I'd better be going. Thank you for the coffee, Priscilla."

She caught her breath. Gerald wasn't the type to be given to flowery words and excessive compliments, which could only mean she made him every bit as flustered as he sometimes made her. Somehow, knowing that made her feel better.

She rose and followed him into the hall, then handed him his coat and stepped back while he shrugged into it. "I'm really glad you stopped by, Gerald."

"Me too." He pulled the zipper up, then let his hands fall to his sides. "I'll call you after I've looked through my reports."

"Okay." She thought for a moment and then held up her hand. "Will you give me just one more second?"

"Sure."

Priscilla hurried to the kitchen, picked up the odd knife from the suitcase, and carried it back to Gerald. "While you're at it, would you mind finding out what you can about this? I sure am curious to know if it's as old as you think."

He took the knife from her. "I'd be happy to."

"Thank you." She shifted her weight to her other foot. Here it was, that awkward moment between two people who were too close for handshakes but not quite more than friends.

He smiled and tipped his head before reaching for the knob. "See you later, Priscilla."

"Bye, Gerald."

She waved and then watched him stride down the walk to his truck. It was strange, being friends with an attractive man. Throughout her many years of marriage, she'd taken care to guard her thoughts and her reputation by only forming deep attachments with other women. Men were reserved to amiable acquaintances only, with the rare exception of couples that she and Gary socialized with together. It was her way of protecting her marriage, and before he died, Gary had told her how much he always appreciated knowing his heart was safe with her.

But now things were different.

Her life here on the island was different. And even though she still couldn't quite convince her head, her heart already knew Gerald was special. And not just in the isn't-he-a-nice-guy kind of way.

Sighing, Priscilla closed and locked the door. She needed something constructive to occupy her thoughts. A good start would be digging for a little more information on the things she and Gerald had found in that suitcase. Flipping her computer on, she began by searching for sites that advertised maps like the one they'd found. It was menial, painstaking work, but it kept her thoughts focused where they should be—on the mystery at hand.

And off of Gerald O'Bannon.

## CHAPTER THREE

Priscilla slid her arms into her coat and zipped it as she stepped outside her cozy cottage. A sharp wind whipped off of the Atlantic, stirring the waves into frothy white tips that stood in stark contrast to the gray water and grayer sky overhead. The snow was still holding off, but the temperature had dropped at least ten degrees since yesterday, and she feared Gerald had been right that their mild days would not hold out much longer.

Shivering, she hurried off the porch and scrambled down the walk to her car. Her fingers shook as she jammed the key into the ignition, rolled the engine over, and turned the heater to High. Maybe one of these days, she would invest in a new car—something with a remote starter like the one her cousin Trudy drove.

She blew into her hands. Someday. For now, she could at least invest in a warmer pair of gloves. Except for the fact that the ones she wore had been a gift from Gary, she would have done it long ago.

Startled by the ringing of her phone, Priscilla fumbled to find it among the clutter inside her purse. She checked the screen, then smiled when she saw her cousin's name displayed, and hit the Answer button.

"Hi, Gail."

"Good morning. What are you up to?"

"Um..." Priscilla glanced at the photos she'd tucked into the front pocket of her purse. Her plan had been to swing by the Coast Guard station to see if Gerald had found anything in his reports regarding a missing boat and then ask around town about the photos. "I'm just heading out, actually."

"On your way for coffee? I have the day off from the dental office. I could meet you at Candy's."

Priscilla's spirits fell. She would have loved meeting Gail for coffee. "I'm sorry, Gail. I was just on my way to see Gerald."

"Gerald, huh?" A smile warmed Gail's voice. "Well, I wouldn't want to keep you from that."

"It's not what you think," Priscilla said, reaching for the photos. Boy, was that an understatement. "He's just checking into some reports for me."

"That's too bad," Gail teased. "I was hoping it was something else. Well, never mind. I'll catch you another time."

Priscilla turned the heater down just a touch so she could hear her phone better. "Are you sure you don't mind? I know it's been several days since we've been able to get together. I'm starting to think I'm going to have to make an appointment to have my teeth cleaned just so I can see you."

"No worries—though I'll be happy to clean your teeth." Gail giggled. "I'll talk to you later. Have fun."

Gail signed off with a light laugh, and Priscilla mentally noted to make an extra effort to set aside some time to spend with her cousins. Though she chatted with one or another of them almost every morning by phone, time and loss had taught her one thing—never to take advantage of the special relationships with those she loved.

She studied the photos for a long moment, trying to glean something about the people and their past before replacing the pictures and her phone inside her purse. Then, mindful of the gusting wind, she drove to the Coast Guard station where Gerald served as a captain.

As always, Priscilla was impressed by the pristine beauty of the stately white buildings, especially the main building with its gleaming cupola. Seeley, one of the many coast guardsmen she'd met since moving to the island, passed her on the road. She offered a smile and a wave before turning into the parking lot and pulling alongside Gerald's white SUV with its distinctive red stripe.

Inside, business seemed to have slowed to a crawl now that the summer tourists were gone. Another coast guardsman named Chickie sat in front of his computer, engrossed in a game of Solitaire. Catching sight of her, he raised his coffee cup in greeting.

"Morning, Mrs. Grant. You looking for the captain?"

Priscilla nodded and approached the long, low counter stacked with computers and monitors where Chickie sat. "Yes, I am, but I don't have an appointment. Is he very busy?"

Before Chickie could reply, Gerald stepped from the glass walls of his office. A smile spread across his face upon spotting her. "Priscilla? I thought I heard your voice."

He handed Chickie a stack of manila folders, then crossed to her. For a quick moment, she wished he had handed one of those folders to her. She could have used it to fan away the warmth that sprang to her face when she saw him in his trim navy slacks and tailored Coast Guard shirt.

She gave herself a mental shake and clutched her purse tighter to her side. "I'm sorry I didn't call first. Is this a good time? I can come back later."

"No problem at all. Come on in."

Gerald motioned toward a kitchen just to the left of his office. Cabinets painted in glossy Coast Guard blue lined one wall, and sitting atop the counter was a pot of fragrant coffee. "Can I get you something to drink? I've got a fresh pot brewing or there are bottles of water in the fridge."

"Coffee would be nice."

"Coming right up."

Gerald filled a mug for each of them and then led Priscilla into his office. His desk hugged one wall, with the two leather chairs that sat opposite facing a bank of windows and the breathtaking view outside.

He waved to one of the chairs. "Have a seat."

"Thank you, Gerald."

Mindful that she'd bordered on rude the last time they spoke, Priscilla made quiet small talk before launching into her reason for coming. But when she got around to asking how Aggie was doing, Gerald laughed and shook his head.

"It's no good, Priscilla. I know you're dying to ask me. Go ahead."

Her shoulders slumped. "Was I that obvious?" She joined in his laughter, setting her cup on the corner of his desk, then leaned forward to rest her hands in her lap. "I know you said you'd call, but I just couldn't wait to hear what you found."

Humor crinkled the skin around his eyes, adding charming character to his already handsome appearance. He pointed to the telephone. "I was actually just leaving you a voice mail when you came in."

"Oh?" And then, with her shoulders slumping again, she added, "Oh. That's bad. Nothing, huh?"

Judging by the fact that he'd merely left her a message, she assumed he had not discovered anything that would lead them to the owner of the mysterious suitcase. She was right.

The humor melted from his face, and he shrugged. "I'm sorry, Priscilla. I know you were hoping I'd have more information to give you, but I didn't find any clues as to where that suitcase might have come from." He reached across his desk and pulled a folder toward him. "This is a log of all the calls that came into the station over the past week. I even went further back a few days, just to be sure I hadn't missed something."

Priscilla eyed the file skeptically. "That's all of the calls? It's a pretty thin file." Realizing how she'd sounded, she put her hand to her mouth and widened her eyes. "Oh, I didn't mean—"

He chuckled and lifted a hand to stop her apology. "It's okay. Fortunately for us, things slow down after the summer season, when the tourists head back to the mainland and most of the boat rental places close down. It's mostly local fishing boats we have to worry about now, and every now and then a rare call from one of the ferry services."

"Ferry services," Priscilla repeated, tapping the handle of her cup. Could the suitcase simply have fallen off one of the ferries? She'd meant to call them earlier and forgotten all about it. She tucked the thought away to ponder later. She pushed her hair behind her ear and jumped to her second reason for stopping by. "Thank you anyway, for checking. I'm really glad the suitcase didn't come from a capsized boat."

He nodded. "Me too."

"What about the knife? Any luck there?"

"Not yet, but I'm hoping to hear something soon." He gestured toward his computer. "I took a picture of it and sent it to some of my Coast Guard buddies. I'm hoping one of them will be able to help me out."

"Okay." Priscilla smiled contritely. "Thanks again, Gerald. I know I don't sound like it with all of these questions, but I really do appreciate your help."

He gave a dismissive wave. "No problem. I'm just as curious as you to find out where that thing came from." He reached for his cup, took a drink, and then crossed his legs and balanced the cup on his knee. "So? What's the next step?"

"Next . . . step?" She raised her eyebrows innocently and took a sip of her coffee.

This time, Gerald laughed outright. "You've proven to be quite the amateur sleuth. I can't imagine you not trying to figure out where that suitcase came from. So? What's the next step?"

*Hmm.* Apparently he was getting to know some of her quirks. That fact both delighted and scared her a little, so rather than address it, she answered his question. "I did do a little sleuthing last night. I found out that the map of Martha's Vineyard that was in the suitcase is unique to the island—so we know whoever bought it was on the island at some point. And the truth is, you sparked an idea just now."

"*I* did?" He leaned forward, his chair muttering a protest, and fixed her with a curious stare. "What'd I say?"

"You mentioned the ferries."

Before she could finish, Gerald's phone rang. He held up his finger, grabbed the phone, jotted down a quick note, and then hung up and motioned for her to continue. "Sorry about that. Please, go ahead. You were saying something about the ferries?"

Warmth flooded her chest. Gary used to do exactly the same thing. She always knew he'd been listening when they talked, because no matter what kind of interruption came, he always prompted her to pick up right where she'd left off.

Her throat felt thick and tight, but she managed to regain her composure. "I was just saying I thought it might be possible that the suitcase came off of one of them."

He nodded. "Absolutely. People lose things on ferries all the time."

"And just as many pedestrians ride across to the island as do people who drive their cars," she continued, her excitement returning. "So maybe I'll call the local ferry companies and see if anyone has complained about missing luggage."

He tapped his temple with his index finger, and his eyes gleamed appreciatively. "That's good thinking, Priscilla. Do you need any help?"

"I don't think so. Not at the moment, anyway. I'll let you know if my questions don't turn up any leads." She took another drink, then stared down into her cup and frowned. "You know what this coffee needs?"

He looked down at his own cup and then back at hers. "I'm sorry. I didn't even ask if you drink yours black. Would you like some sugar?"

"Do chocolate chip cookies count as sugar?"

He laughed and shook his head. "Sorry, Priscilla. I only make one trip per week." He reached behind his desk and lifted a brown paper bag. "Today is sack lunch day."

"Ah, well." She took one last sip of her coffee and set the cup aside. "Gail called this morning. I suppose I'll just have to share my cookie craving with someone else."

"Are you sure?" His lips rose in a teasing grin as he gave the bag a jiggle. "I brought peanut butter and bananas."

She puckered her lips. "As tempting as that sounds…" She shook her head. "Never mind. It doesn't sound tempting at all." She laughed and rose to her feet. "But thank you anyway."

He stood with her. "Too bad. I was looking forward to sharing my sandwich."

She lifted her finger in the air. "Who was it that was famous for liking—?"

"Elvis," he said before she could finish, and shook his head. "I know. My kids pick on me all the time. But what can I say? He was on to a good thing."

Priscilla said goodbye and was still smiling when she climbed into her car. When she arrived at the Candy Lane Confectionery a short time later, she wasn't surprised that she had to drive around several times before she found a parking spot. Even in the off-season, people clamored for Candy's baked goods, though the number of cars packed into the parking lot today was particularly high.

Priscilla wound through the rows of parked cars, dodging bumpers and side-view mirrors, and made her way inside, where she was immediately greeted by the scent of coffee and sweet vanilla. She paused in the doorway, closed her eyes, and took a deep whiff.

"Priscilla, over here." Mildred Pearson, the caretaker of the East Shore Historical Museum, waved to her from a table near the window.

"Mildred?" Priscilla blinked and for a half-second was tempted to rub her eyes. "Is that you? Where are your clothes?"

Several people glanced her way, and Priscilla realized she'd spoken much louder and used words with a far different meaning than she'd intended.

With a wry grin, Mildred looked down at her blue cotton T-shirt and faded denim jeans. "Hopefully, I'm in them—although I've been known to have a dream now and then that I left home in my pajamas."

Priscilla shook her head in embarrassment as she walked over to meet Mildred. "I'm so sorry. That's not what I meant at all. What I meant to say is where is your period costume? No ball gown today or Amelia Earhart aviator jacket?"

Mildred's chin rose proudly. "Not today. I'm painting one of the rooms in the museum, so I opted for more practical attire."

"Painting? In December?" Priscilla slid out a chair, hung her purse on the back, and then sat down.

Mildred's gray head bobbed. "The summer months are far too busy for me to tackle a project like this. Besides, I need something to keep me busy in the off-season months." She picked up a crème horn from her plate and took a bite. "Mmm...these are even better than usual. You should try one."

Flakes from the crème horn fluttered to the plate. Mildred picked a few crumbs off her lips and then brushed the rest away with a napkin. If that wasn't advertisement enough to try one of Candy's flaky crème horns, Priscilla didn't know what was.

"Actually...I think I will." She pointed to Mildred's coffee cup. "Do you want me to get you a warm-up?"

Mildred shook her head, so Priscilla went to the counter and placed her order, then returned to her seat.

"So what exactly is it that you're painting?" Priscilla's eyes widened, and she laid her hand on Mildred's arm. "Not the parlor, I hope. It's so pretty just the way it is. I love that gold and green wallpaper with the plum-colored trim at the top. It's like something out of *Gone with the Wind*."

Mildred took a swallow from her cup and then pressed a napkin to her mouth. "Don't worry. I don't have any plans for changing the parlor." Her lips pursed, and she tilted her head as though thinking. "Though I must say, the crown molding in there could definitely use some freshening up."

"Oh dear. I hope I haven't given you any ideas," Priscilla said, laughing.

Mildred laughed too. "That's all right. I have plenty of my own. No, I thought I would concentrate on the dining room this time around, maybe add a splash of yellow to contrast with those plum-colored curtains."

Priscilla nodded appreciatively. "Ooh, yellow would be pretty. Reminds me of those Southern plantation-style homes you see in all the magazines. And it would match the outside of the museum too."

"Exactly." Mildred pulled a paint sample from her purse and showed it to Priscilla. "Once I leave here, I'm heading to the hardware store to purchase some paint. The only thing I haven't decided is if I want to paint the window frames in that room white to contrast with the walls or leave them natural."

Priscilla's coffee arrived. She added a packet of sugar and a spoonful of cream while she thought. Finally, she tapped the spoon against the rim of her cup and shook her head. "Honestly, I think either one would be beautiful. Those large casings at the top and moldings on the side are such a showpiece. But aren't you worried about taking on such a big project all by yourself? That room is almost twice the size of my living room. Why don't you get your son to help you, or hire someone to do it for you?"

Mildred's chin jutted, and her eyes flashed with spunk. "Why would I do that? I'm perfectly capable of handling a paintbrush."

"Of course you are," Priscilla said quickly, setting down her cup. "I'm just concerned because those ceilings are so high. Aren't you afraid of falling off a ladder?"

"Nonsense," Mildred said firmly. She rested her elbows on the table and braced her coffee cup between her hands. "I admit, I'm not as spry as I was twenty years ago, but I can still finagle a ladder when need be."

One could hardly argue with that. Mildred had more energy than most people half her age. Priscilla shrugged. "Well, just promise you'll be careful."

Mildred agreed with a nod and then motioned to Priscilla. "That crème horn isn't going to eat itself, you know."

Priscilla chuckled and promptly took a bite.

"So what have you been up to lately?" Mildred continued. "Your daughter hasn't talked you into moving back to Kansas, has she?"

"No," Priscilla said, brushing the crumbs from her fingers with a laugh. "I'm quite comfortable here."

"I'm glad to hear it." Mildred's eyes twinkled as she studied her. "I've rather taken a liking to you." She lifted her cup and took a delicate sip.

Priscilla watched her through lowered lashes. Honestly, Mildred was a study in contrast—on the one hand, so reserved and proper, and on the other, strong and determined. Maybe someday the same would be said about Priscilla, but right now? It had taken a traumatic, life-changing event to shoehorn her out of Kansas, and there were *still* moments when she wasn't convinced she'd made the right choice.

Mildred finished her coffee, left a tip on the table, and then rose. "Well, I'm sorry I can't stay and visit longer, but I'd better get a move on if I want to get started on that dining room. Stop by and see what you think of it after I finish."

"I'll do that," Priscilla said and smiled. "Have fun."

Mildred put on her coat, then wrapped a cheery yellow scarf around her neck and was off with a wave. Priscilla heaved a sigh at the whirlwind she left in her wake. Where Mildred got her energy from was a mystery. Eyeing the remainder of the crème horn she'd ordered, Priscilla pinched off a piece and popped it into her mouth. Maybe it was the crème horns!

Candy Lane, owner of the popular confectionery, circled the counter with a coffeepot in her hand. "Morning, Priscilla. More coffee?" She held up the pot.

"None for me," Priscilla said, wiping her hands on a napkin. "I've had two cups already this morning. Any more, and I'll give myself the jitters."

Candy's laugh was charming and sweet, just like her shop. "Chatting with Mildred?"

Priscilla nodded. "She was telling me about her next project. She's painting one of the rooms at the museum."

Candy set the pot down with a thump and slid into the chair Mildred had vacated. "Not the parlor? That room is perfect just the way it is."

Priscilla laughed. "I said the same thing."

She described what Mildred had planned, and when she finished, Candy's gaze circled the bakery.

"Hmm. I wish I had Mildred's energy. This place could use a bit of freshening up."

Priscilla flashed her a sly glance. "You could always hire that handsome new fiancé of yours to help. I hear he's awfully clever with a paintbrush."

Candy was engaged to Beau Ortmann, local contractor and handyman extraordinaire. Her joy shone in her twinkling eyes at the mention of him. She fingered the checkered tablecloth, her cheeks flushing a pretty shade of pink. "I could, but Beau has been pretty busy helping me with plans for the wedding." Excitement snapped in her gaze. "Did I tell you that he picked out a spot for our honeymoon?"

"No." Priscilla pushed her cup aside and leaned in closer. "Where are you going?"

Candy's smile could have lit the room. "We're going to Sugarcreek."

Priscilla drew back in confusion. "Sugarcreek. As in . . . Ohio?"

At the look of surprise on Priscilla's face, Candy laughed outright. "I know. It's not exactly the *first* place I would have chosen, but Beau has a cousin there who owns a bed-and-breakfast. He offered to let us stay a whole week for free."

Memories of her honeymoon with Gary flooded Priscilla's mind, and she smiled, despite the happy ache in her heart. "Oh, Candy, that sounds perfect."

She nodded excitedly. "And we're going to tour some of the Amish farms, go to one or two wine and cheese tastings, maybe check out some of the local shops, all kinds of things. Beau has our entire itinerary planned out."

Priscilla squeezed her hand. "I'm happy for you, Candy."

"Thank you. Between the store and Beau's job, we're both so busy. I'm actually looking forward to getting away to somewhere quiet and peaceful."

"Well then, it sounds like Sugarcreek is just the ticket."

"I hope so." Candy took another look around the shop. "But between running the bakery and planning a wedding, I won't have time to tackle any painting projects anytime soon."

"Maybe you could hire Mildred," Priscilla said.

Candy laughed and made to rise. "Maybe."

Thinking quickly, Priscilla stayed her with a wave and reached for her purse. "Candy, wait. I know you're busy, but could you spare one more moment? I'd like to show you something."

"Of course. I always have time for you." Candy signaled to the girls behind the counter and then settled back in her chair. "What is it?"

Priscilla removed the photos from her purse and laid them on the table. "Do any of these people look familiar?"

Candy squinted to examine the photos and then frowned. "I don't think so, but these pictures kind of make it hard to tell. Why are they so small? Don't you have anything a bit larger?"

"Unfortunately, no," Priscilla said and then went on to explain where she'd gotten the photos.

While she listened, Candy's eyes rounded in disbelief. She looked down at the pictures and back at Priscilla. "Wait...so a suitcase washed up onto your beach, and these photos were inside?"

"Along with a few other things." Priscilla counted the items off on her fingers. When she finished, Candy set the photos down and shook her head.

"I've heard of some strange things washing up onto shore before but never a suitcase. Did you talk to Gerald about this?"

"I did, but he said there haven't been any distress calls reported for over a week. That pretty much rules out a capsized boat."

She put the photos away and then reached for her coffee cup. Even though she hadn't asked for any more, Candy filled it almost absently.

"You know, that suitcase could have been lost over a week ago." Candy rubbed her thumb thoughtfully over the handle of the coffeepot and tilted her head to one side. "I mean, if the suitcase is as banged up as you say, it might have been missing much longer than you think."

"I'm not sure," Priscilla said, raising her eyebrows doubtfully. "It wasn't completely buried, and people walk along that section of beach all the time. Surely someone would have seen it and reported it before now."

"That section of beach, yes, but there are several stretches along the shoreline that are pretty rocky. That suitcase could have been trapped between some rocks for several weeks and only now broken free and washed up outside the lighthouse. With the tides and currents, who knows how long it's been bumping along, waiting for someone to find it?"

Priscilla framed a response and then pressed her lips shut. Candy was right. The suitcase could have been missing for much longer than she'd anticipated. She might have to adjust her thinking to fit an extended timeline.

She wrapped her hands around her cup, letting the heat from the coffee urge the cold from her fingers. "You're right, Candy. I hadn't thought about that. I'll have to talk to Gerald and see what he thinks." She patted her purse. "In the meantime, I think I'll show these photos around town and see if anyone recognizes them."

"Hmm. Well, good luck," Candy said.

Priscilla had brought her cup to her lips, but when she spotted the skeptical look on Candy's face, she set it down without drinking. "What? It shouldn't be too hard, right? I mean, I know the photos are small, but I can always try enlarging them on my computer." She frowned. "Though that might make them a bit grainy."

"No, it's not that," Candy said.

"You're thinking it will take me too long to show them all around the island?" Priscilla waved her hand dismissively. "I'm not worried. There aren't that many tourists on the island this time of year." Candy sucked in a breath, sharp enough that Priscilla narrowed her eyes at her. "What don't I know? What haven't you told me?"

"It's just…" Candy blew out the breath and flashed a smile of apology. "I'm sorry, Priscilla. I seem to be the bearer of bad news this morning."

Priscilla winced and braced herself. "Do I even want to know what you're thinking?"

Candy grimaced. "It's just… there *weren't* many people on the island, but next week is when Christmas in Edgartown starts."

Priscilla relaxed into her chair. "Oh, I've already thought about that. I'm going to take the photos around town today and maybe tomorrow. I'm sure I'll have an answer by then."

Candy shook her head stubbornly and gave a wave that encompassed the bakery. "No, Priscilla. People have already begun arriving. Why do you think the bakery is so full?"

"I just assumed—" Priscilla followed her gaze around the room. Certainly, the parking lot had been full, but she'd thought it was all locals. She put her hand to her mouth. "Oh dear."

Candy's head bobbed. "So you may have more work cut out for you than you think. I'd offer to help, but between the wedding and—" She spread her hands wide and threw a quick glance around the crowded bakery.

"Don't worry about a thing. I completely understand." Priscilla reached for her purse. "And I've taken up enough of your time. Thanks for your help, Candy."

"You're welcome." She rose and grabbed the coffeepot, then paused and scratched her temple. "You know, maybe you should talk to Mildred about the suitcase. If it's as old as you say, she might be able to tell you something about that knife."

Priscilla nodded. "I'll talk to her after I hear from Gerald. Thanks again, Candy."

"No problem."

Candy scooted back to her customers, and Priscilla headed back to her car. Several ferry companies serviced Martha's Vineyard, but one of them was so close that driving to it would be easier than calling. As she drove, she thought about what a difference just a few short months had made. There was no need for her GPS now. She knew her way around. That alone was astonishing, but even more amazing was how many places had a special significance—the shops, the cafés, the museums. They were all combining to make the Vineyard feel like home. But the Steamship Authority terminal was one of Priscilla's favorite places on the island.

She pulled into the parking lot of the pretty gray and white building. As far back as she could remember, the place had welcomed visitors to the island, and had in fact welcomed her on her first visit. The barrels that lined the bricked sidewalk looked empty and forlorn today, now that they were devoid of the flowers that bloomed there earlier that summer. She consoled herself with the knowledge that soon enough, they would brim with Christmas finery. Lights would twinkle from the dock onto the water, and gaily colored ribbons would festoon the windows and doors. She couldn't wait to take it all in.

An embarking ferry gave a blast of its horn. Hearing it, she couldn't help but smile. She still remembered stepping from the ship onto the dock as a child and being greeted by the call of the seagulls and the scent of fish and salty sea air. Today, those same calls beckoned as she left her car and headed toward the ticket office.

A fancy sensor had been installed on the terminal doors. They whooshed open as she neared and invited her to step into the welcome warmth inside. Blinking against the contrast from the brightness outside to the dimmed interior, she paused to get her bearings.

Across from the door, visitors milled around a large rack stuffed with pamphlets touting things to do on the island. Opposite her, a long line formed at the ticket window, but a few feet away, a cheerful-looking woman with graying hair and warm brown eyes sat behind a low desk bearing a sign that read Help/Information. Priscilla headed there.

The woman's smile broadened as she saw Priscilla approaching. She pushed aside a tall stack of pamphlets and maps and greeted her with a nod. "Good morning. Welcome to Martha's Vineyard. Can I help you find something?"

Priscilla couldn't help herself. She flashed a jaunty smile and said, "Actually, the something has already been found. I'm hoping you can tell me who it belongs to."

The woman's good humor melted into befuddlement. She put her hand to her ear as though she hadn't quite heard right and said, "I'm sorry, what was that?"

Priscilla ducked her head in apology. "I should probably explain. My name is Priscilla Grant. I own the lighthouse in Misty Harbor."

"Oh, you're *Marjorie's* niece." Obviously someone who did a lot of talking with her hands, the woman threw her palms high and then brought them down on the desk in excitement. "I heard you moved to the island. Sorry we haven't met before now." She leaned over the desk and stuck out her hand. "I'm Ethel Wallace. Please, call me Ethel. Your aunt and I knew each other for years."

Priscilla shook her hand. "It's a pleasure to meet you, Ethel. And please call me Priscilla."

"It's a pleasure to meet you too, Priscilla." Ethel's fingers fluttered up to her mouth. "Goodness, you look so much like your aunt."

Priscilla's hand rose instinctively to touch her hair. "Really?"

"Oh, yes. I see it in your eyes. And you have her smile too. So bright and pretty. She was such a joy to be around."

"That's nice to know. Thank you, Ethel."

Ethel's head bobbed as she sank back into her seat. "So what is this about you finding something?"

Priscilla explained about her discovery, leaving out the details of what had been inside the suitcase and only touching on where along the beach it had been found.

"So, in short, I'm looking for the owner of the suitcase," she finished. "Do you think it's possible that it could have fallen off one of the ferries?"

Ethel pressed her hand to her wrinkled cheek. "Goodness, I don't know. I suppose it's possible." She thought for a second and then held up a finger. "Just a minute. We have a form that people can fill out when they lose something or leave something behind on one of the boats. I'll look through them and see if anyone has reported missing a suitcase."

She rose and disappeared through a large wooden door marked Private. While she waited, Priscilla took in her surroundings, some of them familiar from her days spending summers with her aunt. Those days seemed very long ago now, and she wondered if the children she saw hanging tightly to their parents' hands would one day look back with the same longing and nostalgia she felt.

Ethel returned some ten minutes later, and by the apologetic look on her face, Priscilla assumed she'd been unsuccessful.

Ethel clasped the gold necklace around her neck and twirled the length of it around her finger. "I'm really sorry, Priscilla. I checked the records twice, but there wasn't anything in them about a missing suitcase."

Somehow she hadn't really expected the answer to be that easy. Priscilla shrugged and hiked her purse strap onto her shoulder. "That's all right, Ethel. Thank you very much for looking."

"Not a problem." Ethel's lashes fluttered, and then she put her fingers to her lips. "Before you go, maybe I should get a phone number from you and a description of the suitcase, just in case someone does turn in a claim."

"That's probably a good idea." Priscilla gave her the information and then tapped her fingernails on the desktop, thinking. "Ethel, do all the ferry companies have a similar policy regarding their lost and found?"

"I suppose." She gave a firm nod of her head. "Yes. At least, all of the ferry services that are run by the Steamship Authority. There are a few private charters that could be different."

Ethel snapped her fingers. "You know, come to think of it, I bet you could ask Almeida Charier about the policy on board some of the other boats. Do you know Almeida? She pilots one of the ferryboats."

Ethel kept talking and waving her hands, but Priscilla had stopped listening at "private charters." She hadn't even considered them. She frowned. Her list of places to call just got longer.

After a moment, she realized that Ethel had stopped talking and was looking at her with eyebrows raised expectantly.

Priscilla shook herself to attention. "Oh my goodness, I'm so sorry, Ethel. What did you say?"

She smiled jovially. "I asked if there is anything else I can help you with today."

Priscilla dug in her purse and pulled out the photos she'd found in the suitcase. "Actually, there is just one more thing." She laid the pictures on the counter, face up, and pushed them toward Ethel. "I don't suppose any of these people look familiar?"

"Hmm." Ethel squinted at the pictures, held them close to her eyes, moved them farther away, then glanced sheepishly at Priscilla. "One second." She rummaged in her desk and pulled out a bulky pair of bifocals. She held them up, her face reddening self-consciously. "I only use them when I'm reading," she explained.

She balanced them on her nose and then looked again. Finally, she took off the glasses and shook her head. "I'm sorry, I'm afraid those people don't look familiar. Of course, we have thousands of people pass through here every day. Maybe you should ask some of the other staff if they know who they are."

"That's okay. Thanks anyway, Ethel. I'll do that." Priscilla scooped up the pictures.

Ethel waved away her thanks and pointed wryly at the sign in front of her desk. "I'm afraid I wasn't much help."

"Actually, you were a lot of help. I can now cross the Steamship Authority off my list of places to check," Priscilla said brightly. "And I appreciate your effort."

Ethel's face brightened. "In that case, you're very welcome. Good luck finding the owner of that suitcase."

"Thank you. Goodbye."

Priscilla waved and then did as Ethel had suggested and checked with a few of the other staff members at the terminal. She had no luck uncovering the identity of the people in the photos—though one man with a plucky grin said he thought the woman looked like his great-uncle Bob…only without the mustache. Priscilla sighed as she turned for the exit.

Really? His great-uncle Bob? She might have laughed if she hadn't been so disappointed.

A cold blast of air hit her just before she reached the doors, and a tall, boorish looking man wearing a heavy overcoat and a hat pulled low over his eyes barreled through. Priscilla sidestepped just in time to avoid being run over, though another man closer to the counter wasn't quite so fortunate. He looked up askance as he was jostled from behind.

"Sorry," the tall man muttered. "Didn't see you there."

He looked anything but sorry as he elbowed his way through the milling crowd to the information desk. Poor Ethel. She'd have loads of fun dealing with him.

Priscilla's gaze locked with the man who'd been bumped. "Well, he certainly looks like he's in a hurry," she said, offering a hesitant smile.

The man agreed with a nod. "Some people just need to learn to slow down." He set down the ferry schedule he'd been reading and stuck out his hand. "Robert Peterson."

Priscilla took his hand. "Priscilla Grant. It's a pleasure to meet you."

"You too." He paused, and his graying eyebrows bunched as he gestured to the photos in her hand. "Say, did I overhear that you're looking for somebody?"

Priscilla's attention zeroed in on him. "Why...yes, you did." Had he been listening, or had she simply been talking louder than she realized?

He motioned toward the photos. "Mind if I take a look?"

"Not at all."

She handed the photos to him. While he studied them, she took in his appearance. Robert was a tall man, at least a foot taller than her, or it may have been that his erect posture only made him appear so. He wore his hair close-cropped and tidy, much like Gary used to. In fact, he even reminded her of Gary a little, except that where her husband's hands had always shown the wear and tear of farm life, Robert's hands were smooth, his nails clean and neatly trimmed.

After a moment, she cleared her throat and raised her brows. "Do you recognize the people in these photographs?"

Robert squinted and then pointed toward his eyes. "Vision's not so good anymore. Have you got a larger picture I could look at?"

"Sorry, no."

He frowned. "That's too bad."

"Thanks, anyway," Priscilla said.

She started to replace the photos, but Robert held up his hand, exposing a tattoo of an eagle on his forearm. "Hold on. I've got some glasses in here somewhere." He opened the flap of his coat and patted the inside pockets. "Ah, here they are."

Sliding on a pair of bifocals, he leaned forward and tipped his head up slightly to study the pictures. "Look like passport photos."

"What?"

He indicated the size with his thumb and forefinger. "You know, a passport photo? It has to be a certain size and taken with the person looking straight ahead, like your friends there."

Priscilla's gaze dropped to the photos in her hand. "Goodness, you're right. They do look like passport photos. How did you know?"

Robert shrugged. "I used to work in the post office. I'm retired now, but I've issued hundreds of those over my career." He held out his hand. "May I see those again?"

"Of course."

Priscilla handed him the photos and then watched as he tipped his head forward and back while he carefully examined each one through the lenses of his bifocals. Finally, he gave the pictures back and peered at her curiously.

"I don't know those people. Why are you looking for them?"

Priscilla chuckled awkwardly. "It's a long story." And one that she wasn't sure she cared to share with a complete stranger.

Robert ducked his head and jammed his hands into his pockets. "Well, if it helps, I'd say if you find one of those people, you'll likely find them all."

"Excuse me?"

He pointed toward his face. "I've got a thing for eyes. Most people don't notice subtle differences, but I do. All three of the people in those pictures have very similar eyes."

"Maybe they're related?"

He lifted one shoulder. "Could be, I suppose. Anyway, good luck finding them."

"Thank you," Priscilla said, watching as he passed through the exit, his shoulders hunched against the cold.

The moment the door whooshed shut behind him, she took one last glance at the photos and then pushed them down into her purse. She hadn't wanted to admit it in front of Robert, but he was right—the people did bear some striking similarities. Somehow, she sensed that was important, and the sooner she found out why, the better.

## CHAPTER FOUR

The Visitors Center located in the Chamber of Commerce in Tisbury looked as though it might have been a home at one time, with its elegant bay window and dark shutters standing stark against the white siding. Though Priscilla had never been to the Visitors Center before, it was a good place where a tourist who wasn't familiar with the island might have gone to report missing luggage. She maneuvered through the alley that ran alongside the building into the parking lot in the rear and climbed from her car.

Outside, a wide door reinforced her opinion that the building had once housed a family, but inside, a cheerful gift shop with racks of colorful postcards and shelves stocked with souvenirs quickly dispelled the image. Priscilla wound past an older couple browsing a display of keepsake spoons and made a beeline for the checkout counter. A pretty girl with flowing blonde hair and a golden tan greeted her with a smile.

"Hi. Welcome to Martha's Vineyard."

"Hello..." Priscilla squinted to read her name tag. "Ashley."

"Are you looking for something in particular?" The young woman motioned toward the wall on her right. "We have an assortment of maps of the island available over here"—her hand swung to her left—"or if you're interested in taking a guided tour—"

Priscilla held up her palm to stop her before she launched into a pitch about the attractions on the island. "No, no, that's all right. Thank you, Ashley, but I'm not actually a visitor to the island. My name is Priscilla Grant. I own the cottage and lighthouse over in Misty Harbor."

Ashley's eyes brightened, and she pushed a stray lock of blonde hair behind her ear. "Oh, I know that place. I drive right past it on my way to work. Is it true that you're thinking about opening up a museum? I've heard a lot of people talking about it. Most say they can't wait to see inside."

A pleased flush warmed Priscilla's cheeks. It was good to learn that so many people were interested in the lighthouse museum. "That's correct. It's going to be a presentation about the history of the lighthouse and the Latham family members who lived there. In fact, we're hoping to open by next summer. I hope you'll stop by."

Ashley bounced on her toes in youthful exuberance. "I'll do that. I'm really into history. I love all that old-timey stuff."

*Old-timey?*

Priscilla cringed inwardly, thinking what Ashley would make of *her*. "Wonderful. In the meantime, I wonder if you could help me with something."

"Sure, Mrs. Grant. What can I do for you?"

Priscilla looked around the small room. "Is this where a person would go if they wanted to report something missing?"

"Missing?" The furrows on her brow cleared. "Oh, you mean like a lost and found. Yes, we have one of those." She pointed toward a table overflowing with sunglasses, hats, flip-flops, even a set of chattering teeth. "People turn stuff in here all the time. At the end of the summer season, if no one claims the stuff on the table, we get to take it home." She leaned over to rest her forearms on the counter. "I scored a totally awesome pair of Michael Kors sunglasses last summer. It's one of the perks of this job."

Priscilla smiled congenially. "That's very nice. But I don't have anything to turn in. I'm just wondering if anyone has come in looking for something a bit larger, like a suitcase."

Ashley drew back, a look of surprise widening her eyes. "You lost a suitcase?"

"Not me. Someone else lost a suitcase."

"Wow. That's a bummer." She rubbed her freckled nose thoughtfully.

"I thought so too. I found it on the beach outside my lighthouse," Priscilla continued. "This is one of the places I thought a person might go to see if anyone had turned it in."

"Yeah, this is probably where I would go if I lost something in town...but you say you found it on your beach?" She tipped her head to one side. "Hey, doesn't that tour bus go by your place?" Ashley circled the counter and plucked a pamphlet from one of the racks. She examined it a moment and then carried it back to the counter and handed it to Priscilla. "Yeah, here it is. I knew I'd seen something about your lighthouse."

The pamphlet was definitely one of Teresa Claybrook's. It was blue and yellow on one side and listed all of the stops the tour made on the other, including Priscilla's lighthouse.

"Maybe somebody got off the bus, forgot their suitcase on your beach and, I don't know, it got caught in the tide or something," Ashley said.

Priscilla smacked her head with the heel of her hand. "The Misty Harbor Tours. I forgot all about Teresa's Premium Lighthouse Tour. Goodness. It seems every time I stop somewhere to ask about that suitcase, I end up adding to my list of places to check."

She handed the pamphlet back to Ashley, who looked down at it and grimaced. "Sorry about that. You know, you could always bring the suitcase here." She pointed to the overflowing lost and found. "If you don't want to bother looking for the owner, I mean."

Priscilla shook her head. "No thanks. I'll keep looking, but I'll keep that table in mind if I don't stumble onto something in the next few days." She pulled the photos from her purse. "One last thing. Would you mind looking at these photos to see if any of these people look familiar?"

Ashley's nails were perfectly manicured and sported a coat of pretty pink nail polish. She took the photos but only gave them a cursory glance before she handed them back. "Nope. Sorry. We get too many people through here in a day for me to keep track of them all."

"I understand. Thank you for your help, Ashley."

"You're welcome. Hey, will you let me know when the lighthouse opens? I'd love to bring a few friends by."

"I'll do that. Goodbye."

Priscilla waved to her and then ambled outside to her car. She still had all of the other ferry and charter services to call, and now she needed to add Teresa Claybrook's tour company.

Her stomach grumbled, prompting her to glance at her watch. The morning had flown by. It was already half past eleven and almost time for lunch. She could run home. There was plenty of sandwich meat in the fridge and a fresh loaf of bread in the breadbox, but that wouldn't allow her to show her photos to anyone else, and she had been craving the Nautilus Café.

Her mind made up, Priscilla headed for the wharf and the sunny little seaside café nestled there. Just like at Candy's place, several cars packed the parking lot, including a bright blue one she thought belonged to her cousin. She went inside and looked around expectantly. Indeed, Gail waved to her from a table near a window overlooking the docks.

Priscilla hurried over to her. "Can I join you? You're not expecting anyone, are you?"

Gail rose and clasped Priscilla's hands. "Of course you can join me. Trudy's on her way too, but I know she won't mind." She pulled Priscilla into a hug, and when she released her, motioned to one of the chairs. "Have a seat."

"Thank you. Trudy is coming too?"

"Uh-huh." Gail looked at her watch. "Normally, she would have beaten me here, but my last patient canceled, so I got here a little early. Probably a good thing." She motioned around the crowded restaurant. "I don't think we'd have gotten a table otherwise."

"Well, I'm so glad I decided to stop here instead of heading home. Lunch with my cousins—what a wonderful surprise." Priscilla smiled as she shrugged out of her coat and draped it over the back of her chair. Spending time with her cousins was one of the many blessings God had bestowed on her since leaving Kansas. She missed her friends back home, of course, and Rachel too, but she was enjoying getting to know Trudy, Gail, and Joan.

They both sat, and Gail waved to a waitress, who promptly took Priscilla's drink order and returned with an iced tea for Priscilla and refill of diet soda for Gail.

"So I thought you were meeting Gerald today?" Gail asked, swirling her straw in her soda.

"I did." Priscilla set down her glass of iced tea and tugged the photos from her purse. While Gail studied them, Priscilla explained about the suitcase and the steps she'd taken trying to find the owner.

"But you haven't had any luck, huh?" Gail said, handing the pictures back.

"Unfortunately, no." Priscilla's shoulders slumped. "They don't look familiar to you either?"

"Afraid not." Gail's lips turned down doubtfully. "But those pictures are awfully small. Do you think you could make them larger somehow?"

"Maybe. I thought about scanning them into my computer at home, but I'm not sure what that will do to the quality."

Priscilla put them away carefully and then took another drink of her tea. Their waitress returned with a pad of paper and a pencil and looked at each of them expectantly.

"Are you ready to order, ladies?"

Priscilla held up her hand. "Actually, we're expecting one more, right, Gail?"

Her cousin handed the menu at her elbow to the waitress. "Trudy is coming, but I'll go ahead and order for her, since I know she'll be here any minute." She nodded to Priscilla. "Go ahead."

"Oh, well in that case, I'll have the gourmet grilled cheese and a cup of the clam chowder," Priscilla said, rubbing her hands together eagerly.

Gail thought a second. "That sounds perfect for a cold day. Make it two." She placed Trudy's order too, and when the waitress left, she folded her hands and eyed Priscilla curiously.

"So tell me some more about the suitcase. What are you going to do if you can't find the owner?"

Priscilla grimaced and grabbed a napkin to mop up the condensation collecting on the outside of her glass. "To be honest, I haven't thought that far ahead," she said, sliding her iced tea aside. "It's only been one day, so even though I haven't had much luck, I'm nowhere near ready to give up."

"Of course you're not. You're a Latham."

"I'm a Grant now," Priscilla said, chuckling.

Gail wagged her finger at her. "But you were a Latham first, and Lathams don't quit."

"No, we don't, especially when God plops a problem practically in our laps."

Gail tilted her head and eyed Priscilla across the table. "So...you think this is something *God* placed in your path?"

Priscilla took a long breath while she pondered her reply. "I think that we often miss the things that God is trying to show us through our circumstances." She paused long enough to look her cousin in the eyes. "To be honest, I have no idea if God wanted me to find that suitcase, or if Jake and I just happened to stumble on it, but I do know that it must have belonged to someone. If that someone were me, I would want it back."

"I would too." Worry creased Gail's brow. "But, Priscilla, what if the person who owned that suitcase...well, what if something bad happened to them?"

Priscilla lifted her chin. "All the more reason to find out what happened." She reached out to grip Gail's hand. "I have to know, Gail. At the very least, I have to *try* to find out what happened."

Gail blew out a breath. "All right, so what do you intend to do?"

Priscilla pulled her hand back and pursed her lips thoughtfully. "My plan is to call all of the local ferry services and private charters. If that doesn't work, I'll check with Teresa Claybrook to see if any of her customers left anything behind on one of her tours. After that..." She shrugged and pushed her hair behind her ear. "I'll keep showing the pictures around town until something turns up."

"If you make some copies, Trudy and I could help." Gail motioned around the restaurant. "Three people can cover a lot more territory than one."

Priscilla looked around. Customers crowded nearly every table in the café, and more waited near the door in a growing line. "You're right. I'll make copies as soon as I get back to the cottage."

She sat back in her chair as their waitress arrived carrying their food. Trudy followed on her heels and gave both Priscilla and Gail a quick hug before sliding into her seat.

"I'm just in time, I see."

"Actually, you're a little early, but I knew you would be, so I went ahead and ordered for you. Tuna melt on rye for you, grilled cheese for us." Gail nodded toward their steaming plates. "Shall I bless the food?"

They nodded and bowed their heads while Gail said the prayer. When she finished, Priscilla took a moment to fill Trudy in on everything she'd shared with Gail.

Trudy nibbled one of her french fries while she listened in fascination. Her head bobbed eagerly when Gail told her about offering to help with the pictures. "Yes, of course we can help." She rubbed the salt off her fingers with a napkin and then held out her hand. "Let me see the pictures."

Once again, Priscilla took them from her purse. While Trudy studied them, Priscilla took a bite of her sandwich. Of course, this was no ordinary grilled cheese the staff at the Nautilus served. Smoky gruyère on top of creamy white cheddar and Muenster cheese, smooshed between two slices of seasoned artisan bread and topped with caramelized onions, made for a mouth-watering treat. Gail seemed to be enjoying her lunch just as much as Priscilla was.

She gobbled half of her sandwich and was starting on her chowder before Priscilla had even finished her first bite.

"Do any of them look familiar?" Priscilla asked hopefully when Trudy looked up from the photos. Trudy traveled in much wider social circles than any of the rest of them. If anyone had a shot at recognizing the people in the pictures, it was her.

Trudy shook her head regretfully and handed the pictures back. "I'm sorry, Priscilla, they don't look familiar."

Priscilla hid her disappointment with a smile and a nod. "That's okay. Thanks anyway, Trudy."

Suddenly remembering what Robert Peterson had said, she laid all three photos side by side. "Earlier today, a man I showed the pictures to at the Steamship Authority said he thought he saw some similarities in their facial features. What do you ladies think?"

Trudy squinted and Gail frowned.

"What kind of similarities?"

Priscilla fingered the edge of the first photo. "Around their eyes. Do you notice anything?"

Gail pinched her bottom lip and her brow furrowed in concentration. "Hmm...I guess you could say they look similar. Maybe the *shape* of their eyes or something? What do you think, Trudy?"

Trudy fluttered her perfectly manicured fingers toward the photos. "It's kind of hard to tell with the woman's hair falling over her forehead."

"Yeah, but the two men definitely share some resemblance," Gail said. She took the photos of the men and slid them side-by-side. "See?"

"That's what I thought," Priscilla said.

Trudy nodded. "Yes, I agree. The men definitely look somewhat alike, although this one is much older." She tapped the photo of the man with the beard.

Gail reached out and pulled the photo closer. "I'm not so sure. Facial hair tends to make men look older, in my opinion, but if you put shorter hair on this guy, and took out some of the gray..."

Priscilla tilted her head to view the photos from a different angle. "You're right, Gail. He would look a lot younger with darker hair."

"Wouldn't we all?" Trudy touched her platinum blonde locks. "Which is why I'll never go gray... at least, not so long as my hairstylist lives."

Laughter bubbled from her lips, encouraging Priscilla and Gail to join in. Finally, Priscilla put the pictures away and concentrated on enjoying the rest of her lunch before her grilled cheese got cold.

"So, Trudy, what fund-raiser does the church have you working on now?" Priscilla asked, wiping a spot of clam chowder from her chin with a napkin.

Trudy arched a brow. "What makes you think I'm working on a fund-raiser?"

Gail stole a french fry off Trudy's plate but paused with it midway to her lips. "Aren't you?"

Trudy relented with a laugh. "All right. We just finished collecting Christmas gifts for needy children. Now I'm changing gears and looking ahead to the annual church fund-raiser. To kick it off, I'm having a party at my house next Thursday. You're both invited, of course."

She pointed to a splotch of ketchup on Gail's sleeve, and Gail wiped it away with her napkin.

"The church fund-raiser is months away," Gail said. "Why are you getting started so early?"

"It's never too early to start planning." Trudy chewed a bite of her tuna melt thoughtfully. "Next year's sale needs to be bigger and better than ever before. Fortunately, I've already got some great ideas for making that happen. The tough part is going to be enlisting enough help to pull everything off."

Gail humphed and set her spoon down with a thump. "Honestly, Trudy, this competition with Wesley Chapel needs to stop."

"Why? It's the community that benefits from our little feud," Trudy said with a sniff. "Besides, a little friendly competition never hurt anybody. I think the members of both churches enjoy seeing who can outdo the other."

Gail gave a roll of her eyes and went back to her chowder.

Priscilla's gaze bounced like a ping pong ball between the two cousins. "If it'll help, I'll be happy to look through the cottage for things I can donate to next year's sale," she said.

Trudy set down her fork and leaned toward her eagerly. "Would you, Priscilla? That would be wonderful. We're always looking for donations."

"Of course. I'll be glad to."

Trudy turned to stare expectantly at Gail. After a moment, she looked up, her gaze sliding from Trudy to Priscilla. "What?"

Trudy's lips tightened. "Priscilla is going to look through the cottage for things she can donate to the sale."

"And?"

The two engaged in a staring match. Finally, Gail gave up with a sigh and set down her spoon again. "Okay, fine. I'll start sorting through some things I was going to donate to one of the resale shops."

"Good. Thank you, Gail."

"But you know how Pop can be. He squirrels stuff away for years and never touches it, but the moment you try to give something away…"

"I'm not worried about that. Anything you can dig up will be fine." Trudy picked up her fork and took a dainty bite of her tuna.

Priscilla lifted her hand to her mouth and hid a chuckle. Sometimes it was blatantly obvious the two women were related. In fact, anyone watching would probably have mistaken them for sisters.

"So, Priscilla, you never finished telling me how your visit went with Gerald," Gail said between sips of her soup.

Interest gleamed in Trudy's eyes. She reached for her glass and smiled coyly as she dragged her straw through the ice. "You went to see Gerald?"

Made uncomfortable by the sudden turn in the conversation, Priscilla trailed her spoon along the bottom of her bowl. "Yes. We had a nice visit. I mean, he couldn't help me find the owner of the suitcase, but we still got to discuss some things." She paused and sucked in a breath. "By the way, I should probably tell you that I invited him over for Christmas dinner. I hope that's all right. He's taking some time off next month when his daughter is due, so he ended up having to work on Christmas Day."

She tried to add the last part casually and wound up sounding stilted. Despite that, when Trudy and Gail shared a knowing glance, she couldn't stop more words from spilling from her mouth.

"Anyway, I just don't think anyone should have to spend Christmas alone. It w-wouldn't have been very Christian of me *not* to invite him, right?"

Her speech was coming faster, her tongue stumbling in places and making her sound nervous. Which she wasn't. Not much, anyway.

Trudy reached out and covered Priscilla's hand. "I think it's wonderful that you invited him, Priscilla."

She stopped her worried fidgeting. "Really?"

Gail echoed Trudy's assurance. "We'll have plenty of room and lots of food to go around." Her shoulders hitched and she grinned. "I think it'll be fun. You know, the more the merrier."

Priscilla plucked at the edge of her napkin, tearing off small pieces and dropping them into a pile at her elbow. "What about Joan? Should I mention it to her, just in case?"

"Joan will think it's an excellent idea," Trudy said firmly. She waited until their eyes met and then offered Priscilla an encouraging smile. "And I think Gary would be happy that you're spending the holidays with friends, just in case you're wondering."

"Oh, but..." Priscilla's gaze darted from Trudy to Gail. Both of them nodded in understanding. She blew out a relieved sigh. "Let's hope Rachel thinks so."

"I thought Rachel liked Gerald," Gail said.

"She does...right now. Because he's just a friend."

"You think he might be more someday?" Trudy asked.

Priscilla shook her head. "I don't know. I didn't think so, but the other day..." She bit her lip, searching for the right words to say and only managing a shrug.

"You're still a vibrant woman, Priscilla." Trudy unfolded her napkin and pressed it to her mouth. A lipstick smudge in the shape of her lips marred the napkin when she pulled it away. She bunched it into a ball and tossed it onto her empty plate. "And if your daughter loves you as much as I think she does, she wouldn't want you spending the rest of your days alone any more than Gary would. Don't close yourself off to the possibility of romance."

"Agreed," Gail said, lifting her glass in salute.

Trudy swiveled in her seat and eyed Gail dubiously. "You're one to talk." She flitted her fingers at her. "What about that guy I tried to hook you up with last month?"

"The banker?" Gail sniffed skeptically and lowered her glass. "He wasn't my type." Finished with her chowder, she pushed her bowl away and rested her arms on the table.

"How do you know if you won't at least go out with him?"

Gail's lips pressed into a tight line. Trudy seemed to take the hint and let the subject drop, but Priscilla knew Gail's reluctance when it came to dating wasn't because she hadn't found anyone who was "her type." In fact, it was the opposite. Tommy Townsend was her type, but she was still keeping that a secret.

Rather than speak, Priscilla bit down sharply on the words— and her grilled cheese. It wasn't her place to spill the details of Gail's love life, so instead of letting herself be tempted, she kept her mouth full and her eyes downcast.

Thankfully, Trudy kept the conversation flowing throughout the rest of their lunch with talk of the Christmas concert at the church and the shopping she still had to do for the costumes. Her eyes sparkled as she talked, and Priscilla wondered if maybe somewhere way down deep, she still dreamed of Broadway.

While Gail questioned Trudy about the choice of Carrie Nash to play Mary in the concert, Priscilla eyed a newcomer to the restaurant—a tall man in a heavy overcoat. He took his time crossing to the counter where the owner, Tobin Worthington, was rolling silverware in preparation for the dinner rush. The stranger wore a hat drawn low over his brow, so she could not get a good look at his face, but there was no mistaking his demeanor or the hunched set to his shoulders.

"Hey, I know that man," she said, tapping Gail's arm to catch her attention. "I mean, I don't *know* him. I saw him earlier today at the Steamship Authority."

Trudy looked around curiously. "What man?"

"Over by the counter. I saw him when I was asking questions about the suitcase."

"He doesn't look familiar," Gail said. "Trudy, do you recognize him?"

Trudy craned her neck and squinted. "I can't tell with that hat on. Of course, there are so many tourists on the island right now." She turned her gaze to Priscilla. "Why are you interested in him?"

She shrugged. "He just caught my attention, is all. He seemed to be in quite a hurry."

Suddenly the man straightened and turned from talking with Tobin to look toward the window where Priscilla sat with her cousins. His gaze wasn't what she would consider hard, but it was piercing.

"Trudy, look, look, look," Priscilla said, patting the table hurriedly. "Do you recognize him now?"

"Never seen him before," she whispered, putting her hand to her mouth.

"Me either." Gail looked at Trudy then Priscilla. "And he's all the way across the restaurant."

"So?" Trudy hissed.

"So why are we whispering?"

Trudy shushed her with a wave of her hands.

The man turned back to Tobin, said something that Priscilla could not make out over the hum of conversation going on about her, and then looked their way once more. He gave what appeared to be a nod of thanks to Tobin and then set off for the exit.

Priscilla exhaled in relief. For just a moment, she'd thought he was going to head in their direction—though why that should concern her was a mystery. Dropping her napkin next to her plate, she scraped back her chair and rose.

"Excuse me for just a moment, would you, ladies? I need to ask Tobin something."

Trudy and Gail both gave her looks of surprise, but Priscilla didn't wait to explain. She crossed the restaurant and leaned over the counter toward the owner. "Excuse me, Tobin, do you mind if I ask who that man was you were just talking to?"

He looked up, his eyes wide. "Oh, hey, Priscilla. You startled me."

Realizing her bad manners, she backed up a step and motioned toward the door. "I'm so sorry. I didn't mean to startle you. It's just, I saw you talking to that man who just left and wondered if maybe you knew him."

He shook his head and laid the silverware bundle he'd just rolled on top of the stack at his elbow. "No, sorry, I didn't recognize him."

"Did he give you a name?"

He shook his head again and reached for a clean napkin. "Nope. Why? Is he someone important?"

"Oh, I don't know about that." She fidgeted from foot to foot. So how then was she to explain her interest? "I just happened to bump into him earlier today and found it odd that it should happen twice in the same day."

Tobin chuckled. "Yeah, well, it's not that big an island. People bump into each other all the time. But it's funny you should ask me about him."

"Why is that?" Drawn by the look of confusion on his face, she stepped closer.

"Because that guy was doing the same thing," Tobin said, waving a napkin at her like a flag. "He was asking about *you*."

## CHAPTER FIVE

O f course, he didn't mention anything about running into you earlier today," Tobin continued, rolling a fork and a knife inside the napkin as he talked. "He just asked if you owned the lighthouse over in Misty Harbor."

Priscilla relaxed her clenched hands and her breathing slowed toward normal. "And what did you tell him?"

"I told him yes, but if he was interested in a tour, he needed to contact Teresa Claybrook." He dipped his head and peered at her slyly. "I figured you would rather have her deal with curious tourists than have them poking around your place again."

She managed a weak smile and crossed her arms. "You heard about that, huh?"

"Yeah, well, word travels fast around here. Anyway, I thought I'd do what I could to stem some of the lookie-loos."

"I appreciate that, Tobin. Thank you. I'll let you get back to work now." She took a step toward her table and then turned back. "Lunch was delicious, by the way."

He favored her with a tip of his head. "Glad you enjoyed it."

He reached for another set of silverware as Priscilla walked away, thinking. Was the man he'd spoken to merely a tourist? She wished she could be as certain as Tobin, but something in the pit of her stomach warned otherwise.

Gail sat with her legs over the side of the chair and her arm resting on the back. As Priscilla approached, she motioned to Tobin and then swiveled around. "What was that all about?"

Priscilla shook her head and resumed her seat. "According to Tobin, just a tourist asking about the lighthouse. That would make sense, I suppose, since he was at the Steamship Authority earlier this morning."

Her answer seemed to satisfy her cousins, but Priscilla was still troubled as she made her way home later that day. The man had seemed in such a hurry earlier. Why? And if he was curious about the lighthouse, why hadn't he bothered to talk to her?

A strong gust of wind grabbed the edges of her coat as she walked toward the front door to her cottage. As she battled to close it behind her, she couldn't help but think how the rising wind echoed the storm she'd been battling inside ever since leaving the Nautilus Café.

Jake's happy bark called to her, and she set aside her thoughts to go and let him out of his kennel. His sloppy kisses brought a smile to her face, temporarily dispelling the other thoughts from her mind. When she pushed up to stand, Jake darted toward the living room.

"Jake, where are you going? Don't you want to go outside?"

Jake always wanted to go outside, so when he didn't come running, Priscilla went to check on him. She was surprised to find him sniffing at the suitcase they'd found on the beach.

She knelt beside him and stroked the soft, fluffy fur around his neck. "What's the matter, boy? We already looked inside. There's nothing in there for you." She gave a tug on his collar, but Jake refused to be deterred. Priscilla sighed and tried again with another tug. "Jake, c'mon. Let's go outside."

Still he sniffed at the suitcase, only this time, he added a high-pitched whine and clawed at the corner.

She blew out a heavy sigh. "Fine, I'll let you look, but I promise there's nothing in there for you."

Squatting, Priscilla flipped open the latches and lifted the lid. Jake's excitement built as he shoved his nose down into the bottom and began clawing at the fabric-covered inside.

"Jake, stop that," Priscilla scolded. "You're going to ruin it."

She grabbed his collar again, harder this time, and pulled him away. Jake seemed to sense her displeasure, because he lay down and rested his muzzle on the floor between his paws.

"That's better." She pointed at him sternly. "You stay there. I'm going to go make copies of those photos for Trudy and Gail so they can help me look for the owner of that suitcase."

She rose, half-expecting him to rise with her. Instead, he stayed where he was, his furry ears hanging low. With his tail, he gave one solitary thump against the wood floor. Seeing his dejected display, Priscilla couldn't help but smile. Rachel had put on similar displays when she hadn't gotten her way as a child. Sometimes, Jake was as difficult to deal with as a toddler.

Her cell phone rang, disrupting Priscilla's thoughts. She hurried to the kitchen to answer it. "Hello?"

"Priscilla? It's Joan."

"Hi, Joan."

"Gail told me about the suitcase you found on the beach."

Priscilla bit her lip. Since she'd already told Trudy and Gail, she probably should have made it a point to call Joan. She rested her hip against the counter and fiddled with the plastic tab on her cell phone case. "I'm sorry. I didn't mean to leave you out."

"Oh, that's all right. I wasn't calling to scold you," Joan said with a laugh. "I just wanted to see if you'd found out anything this afternoon. I mean…a suitcase? I've heard of all kinds of things washing up on a beach, but a suitcase is pretty rare. Can't you just imagine that thing bobbing across the Atlantic on its way here from someplace exotic?"

"Exotic?"

"Yeah, like Portugal or Iceland. Places like that."

Priscilla chuckled. "I don't think it came that far."

"You never know." Joan chuckled with her. "And Gail said there were photos inside?"

Priscilla dug in her purse until she found them. "Yes. In fact, Gail and Trudy offered to help me show them around town to see if anyone recognized the people in them. I was just about to make copies."

"Make a set for me too. I'll be happy to help."

Once again, Priscilla was overwhelmed by the generosity of her three cousins. "Thank you, Joan. That's so sweet."

"No problem. So what else was in the suitcase? Anything special?"

Special? Strange, more like it. While Priscilla talked, Joan made small noises but gasped when Priscilla said she'd also found a knife.

"What kind of knife? You didn't touch it, did you? What if it was used in a crime?"

Priscilla pulled out a chair to sit near the table. "Apparently my penchant for solving mysteries is starting to rub off on you."

Joan laughed. "I guess that was a pretty big leap."

"It's not that kind of knife anyway. Gerald said he thought it was pretty old, like World War II era."

"Wow. That is old." The caution returned to Joan's tone. "Still, just because it's old doesn't mean it's not dangerous. You really should be careful."

"You're right." Priscilla straightened in her chair. "I've been so wrapped up in the photos, I haven't given the knife much thought. I probably should check with Gerald to see if he's learned anything new. I'll try calling him this afternoon."

"Will you let me know what you find out? I'm very curious," Joan said, a hint of excitement in her voice.

"Of course," Priscilla replied. "Now, on a different note, are you still planning on coming over for Christmas?"

"Absolutely. Why? Are we changing the plans?"

"No, but we may need to make room for one more. I . . . invited Gerald." Priscilla picked nervously at a loose string on her sweater while she waited for Joan's response.

"Isn't his daughter due around that time?"

"Uh-huh. Well, next month actually, but that's why he decided not to take any time off at Christmas. He wanted to be able to spend some time with Aggie after the baby's born."

"Aww, that's sweet. Well, I'm glad you invited him. Did he say he was coming?"

Relief sagged Priscilla's shoulders. She knew she worried too much what others thought of her choices—a nagging side effect of Rachel's disapproval and her own doubts about selling everything and moving to Martha's Vineyard. Still, she and Gary had been married so long, it was taking a while for her to get used to being on her own and trusting her intuition when it came to decision making.

"I think so. He sounded interested, anyway. I'll let you know for sure as the day gets closer."

"Well, I think it'll be lovely. Is Rachel coming?"

"She is, and I'm so glad. It'll be hard enough spending another Christmas without Gary. I can't imagine Rachel not being here."

Compassion warmed Joan's voice. "I understand completely. All right, well, let me know if I can do anything to help you get ready, okay?"

"Will do. Thank you, Joan."

They said their goodbyes and then hung up.

Before returning to the living room, Priscilla arranged the three photos on the table, took a picture of them with her phone, and sent them via text message to her cousins.

She slid the phone into her pocket. "There. That's one thing off my list."

She headed back toward the living room, surprised that after so much time, Jake still hadn't joined her in the kitchen. Normally he was her little shadow, dogging her steps, as it were, and staying close by her side. The moment she crossed the threshold into the living room, she understood why he hadn't joined her. The naughty dog had climbed *inside* the suitcase and was now clawing his way frantically south.

"Jake, no! Stop that right now." She rushed forward, almost afraid to see what kind of damage he had inflicted to the bottom. Thankfully, though it bore some marks, the material was not yet torn. Priscilla sagged with relief and pointed an accusing finger at the dog. "That was a very bad dog, Jake."

His ears drooped, but he nudged her knee with his nose.

She crossed her arms and eyed him sternly. "Oh no, you don't. You're not coaxing your way out of this one."

He cowered on the floor, as if just the tone of her voice was too much for him to bear.

"All right, you. Let's go. Outside. I'm not taking any more chances."

She didn't give him a choice in the matter but lifted him to his feet and then half-pulled, half-pushed him toward the door. Luckily, Jake wasn't a large dog. She never would have gotten him out of the house otherwise.

Once they reached the door, Jake made a beeline for the backyard, where Priscilla had taken the precaution of setting up an invisible fence. She didn't worry about him running away, but he was still young, and the occasional squirrel had proven to be a distraction she didn't want to battle.

While Jake wandered the yard, Priscilla returned to the living room. Sighing with disgust, she knelt to examine the claw marks Jake had made. She'd have some explaining to do if she ever did find the owner of the suitcase.

Grabbing it by the edges, she rose and carried the suitcase with her to the kitchen. What was it about an empty suitcase that interested Jake? Perhaps there was something she had missed—something less obvious than the strange items she'd found inside.

A false bottom?

Her skin prickled. She'd read of such things, of course, but had never actually seen anything like what her books had described. Still, it was possible. Careful probing, however, didn't reveal the hidden compartment she'd hoped to find. Then again, the pattern of Jake's clawing didn't exactly fit what she would have thought if he'd been digging at the bottom of the suitcase. These marks looked more like he'd been trying to reach something on the side.

Priscilla shifted to examine the suitcase from another angle. Staring straight down into the suitcase, it did seem as though one side bulged outward a little farther than the other.

She crossed to a drawer next to the sink and took out a butter knife. At first, she tried cautiously pulling the fabric sides away from the edge of the suitcase without damaging the leather. When that failed, her attempts grew heartier. Finally, the material gave way with a ripping sound that made Priscilla cringe. She dropped the knife with a clatter.

"Well, so much for Jake scratching up the suitcase," she mumbled. "I did more damage than he did."

Except maybe she had found what Jake was after.

Something small and brown poked out from the hole Priscilla had created. She held her breath as she reached down inside to see what it was.

She pulled out a leather pouch. Heavy. Like it was filled with gold coins or something. Her excitement grew.

It took her a moment to loosen the strings that held the pouch closed. Finally, she worked the knot free and shook some of the contents out into her hand.

"Rocks!" Her disappointment echoed in the empty kitchen. Though she was alone, she looked around anyway, and then lowered her voice. "Why in the world would anyone go to so much trouble to hide a bunch of rocks?"

The question pricked at her as she thought back over the day. She'd made two stops after she left the restaurant—one at the Tisbury Police Department to see if anyone had called about the missing luggage, and one by Ortmann's store on the off chance that the people in her photos had stopped there for groceries. Neither stop proved successful, which meant she still had a busy night of phone calls ahead.

She glanced at her watch. It was a quarter after four, which meant that many of the places she needed to call would be closing soon.

Not pausing to second-guess her decision, Priscilla carried the pouch to the flour bin and deposited it deep inside. Whoever owned the pouch had felt compelled to hide it. Though she didn't know why, she would do the same. Then she went back to the suitcase and put it back together as best she could.

"Well, that's all I can do," she sighed. She took the suitcase back to the living room and replaced the contents before dropping the lid and securing the latches. Afterward, she returned to the kitchen to hunt for a piece of paper and a pen so she could begin looking up phone numbers.

Once she had everything she needed, Priscilla sat down at the table. She still needed to call the local ferry and charter services, but she had Teresa Claybrook's contact information in her phone. While she waited for Teresa to pick up, Priscilla pondered the pouch. Maybe Gail or Trudy would know what the rocks inside were and why the owner of the suitcase had bothered to hide them.

"Misty Harbor Tours, this is Teresa speaking. Can I help you?"

Priscilla turned her attention to the phone. "Teresa, it's Priscilla Grant."

Teresa's voice warmed. "Hi, Priscilla. What can I do for you?"

"Actually, I'm hoping I can do something for you. Have any of your patrons reported missing a suitcase?"

"A suitcase?" Confusion deepened Teresa's tone. "No, I can't say they have. We've had calls about other things, missing phones mostly, but no suitcases. But then, most people don't bring a suitcase on a tour bus. Why?"

As she explained, Priscilla got up and paced the kitchen, every now and then peeking out the window for signs of Jake. At the very edge of the yard, she glimpsed his tail wagging. Though she couldn't see what made him so happy, she was satisfied that he was managing to keep himself entertained and out of trouble.

"So, anyway, Teresa, if anyone does happen to mention a missing suitcase, will you tell them to give me a call?"

"I'll be happy to," Teresa said, and then said incredulously, "I know our island is pretty, but a person would have to be very distracted to leave an entire suitcase behind." She tsked lightly over the phone. "Anyway, I'll let you know if I hear anything."

"Thanks, Teresa."

"No problem." There was a slight pause, and then she said, "Say, how is the museum coming inside the lighthouse? I'm getting ready to print up some more pamphlets for next year's tourist season, and I thought I would add a little blurb about it."

Priscilla pinched her bottom lip. She really hadn't given as much thought to the museum as she should in the last couple of days. "It's coming along," she said. "I found several family photos and a few heirlooms I thought might be interesting to people. I'm also going to see about hanging some of Aunt Marjorie's paintings. Hopefully, it'll all be ready by next summer."

"That sounds great, Priscilla. I'll e-mail you the blurb before I add it to the pamphlet, just so you can look it over before I print them."

"That'll be great. Thank you, Teresa."

Priscilla bid her goodbye and then went in search of her laptop. She would need to look up the numbers for the other places she intended to contact. Rather than calling them one by one, she elected to make a list and then cross the names off as she worked her way down so she didn't accidently call the same place twice. By the time she finished, she had accumulated the names of over twenty businesses.

She flicked the top of her pen against the tabletop. "Well, this is going take me the better part of the afternoon," she muttered as she reached for her phone.

She tapped in the numbers, waited for the phone to ring, and then repeated the same message she'd given to Teresa. Over and over she repeated the process, and each time she received the same answer—plenty of missing phones, hats, sunglasses, and the like, but no missing luggage. When she hung up for the last time, she could almost recite the responses by heart.

*Sorry, no missing suitcases. We'll call you if any information turns up.*

Sighing, Priscilla set the phone aside and rubbed her eyes, then grabbed the pen and crossed off the last business. "Well, Jake, that does it. I'm all out of places to call."

Instead of the thump of a tail or the low-pitched whine she expected, the kitchen hummed quietly.

Priscilla looked around. "Jake?"

He was still outside! She scolded herself as she scooted up from the table and rushed to the door. "Poor dog. I forgot all about bringing him in."

Not that he probably minded. Jake loved being outside, but she had to wonder what condition she'd find her flower beds in. Jake was a dog, after all, and dogs were prone to digging. She stepped outside, wrapping her arms around herself as she searched the yard for signs of his red-and-white coat.

"Jake?"

Normally, he bounded toward her when he was ready to come in. Today, however, he must have found something interesting, indeed, to keep him so occupied. Priscilla moved farther out into the yard.

"Jake, c'mon boy. Time to come in."

Still nothing. Priscilla frowned. She began walking the yard, from one corner of the house to the other. When she didn't spot him, she went around to the side. Worry clutched her heart when, after a thorough circuit of both the back and the front, she still hadn't found him. Had the invisible fence malfunctioned? When had she last checked the batteries on his collar? What if they were dead and she hadn't realized it? She glanced at her watch, dismayed to see that he had been outside, alone, for over an hour.

Priscilla shouted Jake's name until her voice hurt. She searched every corner of the yard again, and when that didn't work, she walked down to the beach, where there was no sign of him. Then she got in her car and drove up and down the roads around her cottage, calling out the window for him, but to no avail.

She pressed her hands to her stomach, trying vainly to quell the flutter of unease and guilt. It was no use. She'd looked everywhere, and now it was time for her to face the truth.

Jake was gone.

## CHAPTER SIX

W hat do you mean 'Jake's gone?'" Gail's voice vibrated with the same concern Priscilla felt, even transmitted across the tenuous strand of an invisible phone line. "How long has he been missing? Did you check the beach?"

"In both directions." Priscilla looked out the living room window, her eyes straining—longing really—for a glimpse of Jake's rust-and-white fur. "I left him outside while I was making all those phone calls yesterday. I forgot about him, Gail. I wasn't worried because of the invisible fence I had installed."

"Of course you weren't worried. That's what the fence is for."

"I still should have checked on him. I'm just sick wondering where he could have gone. I couldn't sleep, so around midnight, I got up and put all of his favorite treats in a bowl in the backyard, then I spent the rest of the night checking to see if he'd come back. I even gathered up all his squeaky toys and walked around squeaking them because I thought maybe he'd hear them and come running back." She squeezed her eyes shut, remembering how Jake had appeared distracted by something she couldn't see.

"Well, on the bright side, this is an island. He couldn't have gotten far, right?"

"I guess not."

"But that's not what you're worried about."

Priscilla sighed. Gail's phone calls had become a welcome ritual. While she enjoyed their talks, she had also learned that there was no hiding her feelings when it came to her intuitive cousin.

She plopped down into a chair at the kitchen table and rested her forehead against her hand. "What if he was hit by a car, Gail? Or worse, what if he got hurt some other way and he's lying in a ditch somewhere waiting for me to find him?"

The thought drove her to her feet and over to the window to check outside. She pushed aside the curtain, not really expecting to see anything but still disappointed when she didn't.

Gail clucked sharply. "Now, now, there's no sense borrowing trouble. Have you called the animal shelters?"

Priscilla let the curtain fall into place. "Not yet. They don't open until nine."

"All right, then. I'll come over and keep you company until they open. And I'll help you make the calls."

Priscilla stopped in her tracks, the knot in her throat loosening with hope for the first time all morning. "Would you, Gail?"

"I'm on my way."

The phone clicked, and Priscilla knew Gail had hung up and was probably already headed toward her car. Despite the worry clutching her chest, she smiled. It was good having family, but it was even better having family who were also friends.

While she waited for Gail to arrive, Priscilla dumped out the remains of her first pot of coffee and put on a fresh one. The action only provided a temporary reprieve from her troubled thoughts, so rather than pace, she shrugged into her coat and went outside. A light dusting of snow had fallen overnight, painting the ground in fresh white canvas. Normally, she would have found the sight beautiful and breathtaking. This morning, she only fretted about whether or not Jake had found shelter from the cold.

She rubbed her hands over her arms, chilled despite her heavy winter coat. "Jake!"

She walked a few steps and then listened fervently for the slightest whisper of his happy bark. Oh, where was that dog? She walked and called until she heard the crunch of Gail's tires in her driveway, and then she rounded the side of the house and waited near the steps to meet her. Gail's face looked troubled as she climbed from the car. She clutched a leash in her hand.

Priscilla waved. Good thinking. When they found Jake, a leash would certainly make walking him home much easier. But as Gail neared, Priscilla realized it wasn't a leash she carried...it was a collar. Jake's collar.

She sucked in a breath that caught painfully in her chest and squeezed. "Where did you find that?"

Gail's lips tightened gravely. She pointed toward the road. "I spotted it lying on the shoulder a ways back."

Priscilla's throat burned, but she forced herself to speak the question sparking the fear in her heart. "Did you see...was there any sign...?"

She shook her head. "No sign of Jake." She held up the collar. "It's not torn, either. It doesn't look like he was hit, Priscilla. It looks like someone took it off."

When Gail had walked up holding Jake's collar, Priscilla had almost expected to see a mangled mess. It relieved her to hear that wasn't the case. She reached for the collar and looked over the entire length of it. "What do you mean 'someone took it off'?"

"Well, the buckle is undone. See?" Gail pointed to the shiny silver buckle. Dangling from it was Jake's dog tag. "It didn't slip over his head on accident. So unless your dog has figured out how to take off his own collar, I'd say someone did it deliberately."

Priscilla gripped the collar tightly, the metal buckle biting into her fingers. "Oh, Gail, surely not. I mean, why would anyone do such an awful thing?"

Gail thought a moment and then ducked her head, her eyes brimming with regret. "You're probably right. There has to be another answer. I only wish I knew what it was." She stomped her feet and blew into her hands.

Priscilla motioned her toward the house. "C'mon. Let's go inside where it's warmer. I've got coffee started for you."

"You're an angel." Gail followed as Priscilla led the way into the house, pausing at the door to remove her wet shoes. "I grabbed the directory listing on my way out the door," she called. "I thought it might be easier to look up all of the animal shelters on the island."

Priscilla headed straight for the kitchen. "I jotted down the numbers for a few too. Maybe you can call the local shelters and I'll call the vets."

Gail joined her in the kitchen. "Sounds like a good plan. Does Jake have a chip?"

Priscilla frowned, her hand hovering over one of the cups next to the coffeepot. "Yes, but that only works if a vet clinic or shelter finds him and scans it. We can't use it to track his location."

Gail laid her hand over Priscilla's arm and squeezed. "Don't worry. We'll find him."

The tension gripping Priscilla's heart eased. She nodded her thanks and then filled two cups with coffee. "Okay, let's get started."

Gail held up her cell phone. "First one to find Jake, wins."

She sounded so enthusiastic, Priscilla couldn't help but smile. A half hour later, her hope had diminished some, since the last number on her list was for a clinic on the other side of Martha's Vineyard. There was little chance Jake had made it there, but she had to try, so she dialed the number and held the phone to her ear while she waited for someone to answer.

"Animal Health Care Associates," a female voice said.

Priscilla had repeated the same words so many times, she knew them by heart. "Hello, my name is Priscilla Grant. I own the lighthouse over by Bailey Point. My dog is missing, and I wonder if anyone there has seen him."

"What kind of dog?"

"He's a mix. He's red and white, and he answers to the name Jake."

"One moment, please."

The voice on the other end of the line became muffled, and Priscilla glanced over at Gail. "Any luck?" she mouthed.

Gail shook her head and covered the end of her cell phone with her hand. "You?" she mouthed back.

Priscilla's eyes burned with tears. She blinked them back rapidly. "Not yet."

At that moment, the person returned. "Ms. Grant?"

"Yes, hi," Priscilla said, turning her attention back to the call.

"A dog was dropped off that matches the description you gave. Would you like to come by and take a look?"

Priscilla sat up so quickly, she upset her coffee cup. Fortunately, it was nearly empty. She dabbed up the spilled liquid with a napkin and tossed it into the trash. "Really? Oh, that's wonderful. How late are you open?" She motioned briskly to Gail. Next to her, Gail disconnected, and her eyes widened hopefully.

"We're open until five," the woman said.

Emotion tightened Priscilla's throat, but she managed to squeak out, "I'll be there before noon." She drew a breath to steady herself before going on. "Do I need to bring anything with me to prove he's mine? He was a stray, so I don't have any official papers, but I have his vaccination record from the vet's office where I got him and a copy of the paperwork I filled out when I adopted him. And he has a chip, so that should identify him as mine."

"That will be fine. We've been very busy since he was brought in and haven't had a chance to check for a chip," the woman said. "We'll see you soon."

"Thank you so much," Priscilla said and hung up the phone.

Gail leaned forward, her face strained but hopeful. "Well? Did you find him?"

"I think so."

Gail let out a whoop and pulled Priscilla into a happy hug—which of course loosed the tears she had been holding back. Soon they were both laughing and wiping away tears.

"He's at Animal Health Care Associates, of all places," Priscilla said, letting out a shuddering breath as she sank back into her seat.

Gail gave a puzzled frown and used a napkin to dry the dampness under her lashes. "That place is like six or seven miles from here. How in the world did he get all the way over there?"

Giving one last sniff, Priscilla jerked to her feet and reached for her coat and the leash hanging on a hook by the door. "I have no idea, but I'm going right now to check. Thank you so much for your help, Gail."

Her cousin grabbed her own coat. "I'm going with you. I need to hear how that crazy dog managed to get so far away." She picked up the collar she'd found on the road. "Not to mention figuring out how he got out of this without help. C'mon. I'll drive."

Navigating the many turns and winding roads in winter made the drive a full twenty minutes. Priscilla had almost resorted to biting her nails by the time they turned off Edgartown Road and down a smaller street toward the parking lot of the Animal Health Care Associates building.

"Well, this is it," Gail said, shoving the car into Park and then unbuckling her seat belt.

Priscilla reached for the door handle. A red-and-white striped awning above a set of glass double doors extended a warm welcome, and as she and Gail trekked up the walk, she released a small bit of the apprehension that had been coiled in her belly. Maybe it hadn't been so bad for Jake here.

She pulled open one of the doors and hurried inside, where she was greeted by a youngish vet tech with shoulder-length brown hair and a pleasant smile.

Priscilla neared the counter and stuck out her hand. "Hello, my name is Priscilla Grant. I called earlier today about a missing dog?"

"Ms. Grant, it's nice to meet you," the tech said as she rose. She took Priscilla's hand in a firm grip. "I'm Mary. I'm the person you talked to."

"It's nice to meet you, Mary." She turned to Gail. "This is my cousin, Gail."

She waited while Gail and Mary exchanged greetings and then took Jake's immunization record from her purse and laid it atop the counter. "So, about Jake?"

"I'm sure you're anxious to see him," Mary said with an understanding smile. She looked over the record from Jake's vet and then pushed it back toward Priscilla. "If you'll wait here a moment, I'll go get him for you."

Though it probably only took a few minutes, the wait seemed to last hours. Gail went to sit on a line of chairs near one of the many low windows, but, unable to remain still, Priscilla loitered near a large metal shelf displaying a variety of dog food and treats. On the walls, posters promoting everything from heartworm medicine to chew toys covered every inch of space. Barking, some high-pitched and some low, carried from behind the door Mary had disappeared through, and Priscilla couldn't help wondering if one of those voices belonged to Jake. She counted the seconds—and the barks—until Mary reappeared with him in tow.

All of the tension Priscilla had been feeling poured from her body in a giant whooshing sigh as she caught sight of her dog's familiar red-and-white fur. "Jake."

Hearing his name, the playful dog yipped, and his tail end began a frantic jig.

"Jake, you bad dog," Priscilla scolded, rushing over to meet him and crouching low to catch him in her arms. She cupped his face in her hands and tickled his ears. "You had me so worried. How in the world did you get all the way over here?"

Jake continued to whimper as he covered her face in wet kisses. Finally, Priscilla had to push him away just so she could stand.

"All right, all right," she said, giving his head one last pat. "All is forgiven." She looked over at Gail, who had witnessed the entire display with a wide grin on her lips. "Can you watch him for me while I fill out any paperwork I need to do?"

"Of course. Come here, you silly dog," Gail said. She lowered to her knees and rubbed Jake's neck playfully while Priscilla followed Mary to the counter.

"Thank you so much for taking care of him," Priscilla said. "I haven't had Jake long, but he's become very special to me. I can't for the life of me figure out how he got out of his collar."

Mary nodded sympathetically. "Did you check the buckle to see if it was broken?"

"I did, in fact." She gestured to Gail. "My cousin found it on the road down from my house. It looked fine."

Mary rubbed her finger over her lips. "Well, dogs can be pretty clever. My little dachshund is the same way. I call him Houdini because he's always finding a way out of the kennel my husband and I built for him last summer. Some dogs really are a lot smarter than most people give them credit for."

"I guess so. I'll be more careful from now on."

"And according to his records, Jake was a stray originally?" Mary continued.

"Yes, that's correct," Priscilla said.

The tech's brow wrinkled as she nodded. "Sometimes dogs that are used to being on their own are more prone to wander. Don't beat yourself up over it." She pulled some paperwork from a manila folder and began flipping through the pages until she found the one she wanted.

"Well, I'm just glad that someone found him and turned him in." Priscilla rested her arms on the counter and tapped a jar of dog treats thoughtfully. "Say, I don't suppose the person who found him left a name? I'd like to be able to thank them and hear where exactly they found Jake so I can figure out where he was going."

"Of course." Mary looked down at the paperwork and then frowned. "Well, that's odd."

Priscilla glanced at the paper in her hand and then at Mary. "What?"

Mary laid the page on the counter and turned it around so Priscilla could see. "It says here that the person didn't actually bring Jake in. One of the other vet techs found him this morning tied to a parking sign outside."

"What?" Priscilla scanned the report as though it might tell her something that Mary had inadvertently left out. "I don't understand."

"You see, we don't normally take in strays," she explained. "Whoever brought Jake in must have known that, but rather than trying to find a shelter that would take him, they tied him to the parking sign, probably because they assumed we wouldn't be able to turn him away."

Thinking of her poor pup shivering outside on the cold pavement overnight cooled some of the gratitude Priscilla had been feeling for the mysterious stranger. She drew her shoulders back and pursed her lips, but spotting a cross necklace hanging around Mary's neck, she forced herself to let go of the anger simmering at the surface and focus on something more positive.

"Well, I suppose they could have done nothing when they found him. And who knows what would have happened to him if he just wandered all over the island. He could have been hit by a car or worse."

"That's exactly right," Mary said, her voice kind and soothing.

Priscilla thought for a second. "You said one of the other vet techs found him. Would you mind telling me who?"

"Not at all." Mary read over Jake's paperwork then pointed at something midway down the page. "It says here that Tyler Phillips found him. He's one of our new guys, only been employed here a few weeks." She smiled brightly. "If you don't mind waiting, I'll go and get him for you."

"That would be great. Thank you."

In only a couple of minutes, Mary returned with a tall, skinny young man in tow. At their appearance, Jake let out a loud bark, but Gail quieted him with a treat from the jar on the counter, so Priscilla returned her attention to Tyler. His hair was cut in the ragged style that seemed so popular now, but that Priscilla's mother had always considered "unkempt."

Mary walked around the counter and introduced Tyler to her. While she spoke, Priscilla noticed that Tyler seemed uncomfortable. He fidgeted with the sleeves on his shirt and did not meet her gaze but kept his eyes fastened on his shoes—a pair of dark brown work boots with scuffs on both toes.

Priscilla stuck out her hand. "It's nice to meet you, Tyler. Thank you so much for taking care of my dog."

"No problem." His gaze darted up to meet hers and then away so quickly, she barely had time to note the color of his eyes—hazel.

"Mary says you found him tied to a sign outside?" she prompted quietly.

He hooked one hand around his arm. "That's right."

"Do you remember what time that was?"

"I come in at eight."

"But I thought the office didn't open until nine."

Tyler fidgeted from foot to foot.

"Tyler comes in early and helps feed the animals and clean cages," Mary explained. "He doesn't have to do it, but he volunteers because he loves the animals. Right, Tyler?" She smiled encouragingly at him, but he didn't smile back. Instead, he turned red, all the way to the tips of his ears.

"Oh, I see. That's very nice, Tyler." Priscilla tilted her head, angling for a better look at his face, but he avoided her gaze skillfully. "Do you happen to know how long Jake had been outside? I mean, did it look like he'd been there a long time?"

"I really couldn't tell," he said. His shoulders slumped as he looked at Mary. "I should get back to work."

"Of course. Thanks, Tyler."

Priscilla had more questions, but having seen Tyler's reaction, she doubted she'd get a straight answer. She waited until he disappeared from view and phrased her next question carefully. "Mary, did anyone else happen to see Jake before Tyler brought him in? I'm just curious if maybe they noticed anything odd that Tyler might have missed."

Mary lifted her hand to tuck her hair behind her ear. "Sorry, no. He was the only one here until nine, when the rest of us arrived."

"But he has a key to the office?"

Mary shook her head. "We don't use keys anymore. All of the doors have keypads, and every employee has their own access code."

"Oh, right." Which meant they could easily check to see what time employees came and went. Priscilla nodded her thanks.

"Anyway, I'm sure you're ready to get your little guy home," Mary said. She smiled and held out the pen for Priscilla to sign the release papers.

When she finished, Priscilla pushed the papers back to Mary and laid the pen on the counter. "Is that it?"

"That's it," the tech said, gathering everything up and tapping the edges against the counter. "Since Jake is up-to-date on all of his shots, there's nothing else you need to do."

"What about paying for his boarding? I really am so grateful that you took him in." Priscilla pulled her wallet from her purse. "I don't mind paying for any food you gave him or any other expenses he incurred."

Before she finished speaking, Mary was already shaking her head. "The doctor said to tell you not to worry about a thing. He's such a sweet dog. All of us here at the office are just glad that he's going home."

Relief filled Priscilla's heart. She grabbed her purse off the counter and placed the strap over her shoulder. "Thank you so much, Mary, and please thank the vet for me as well."

"I'll be glad to," she said. She turned to Jake and wagged her finger at him. "You behave yourself, Jake. Stay home like a good boy."

Jake seemed only too happy to be leaving the vet's office. He gave a bark that echoed against the walls and floor, and bounced on his back legs while he strained toward the door. Gail struggled to hold him while Priscilla buckled on his collar and leash before leading him outside toward Gail's car.

"Home now?" Gail asked.

"I think that's a good idea," Priscilla said. "Maybe I can get someone out to the cottage to take a look at the fence. I don't think I'm going to trust Jake outside alone again until I'm certain the fence is working properly."

Gail hit the unlock button and opened the back door of her car for Jake to jump inside. "That's probably a good idea. I wish I could figure out how he got out of his collar, though."

"Me too." With Jake safely snuggled into the back seat, Priscilla shut the door and climbed into the front. "Did you hear what Tyler said about finding Jake tied to a sign in front of the office?"

"Only some parts. Jake was too wound up for me to catch everything," Gail said. "He sure was an odd fellow."

"I thought so too," Priscilla said, reaching back to grab her seat belt. She pulled it across her waist and locked it in place. "And he kinda reminded me of Rachel when she was little. The way he wouldn't look me in the eyes? Rachel used to do the same thing whenever I caught her telling a fib."

The thought festered as they made the drive toward home. From time to time, Jake laid his head on Priscilla's shoulder, as though to say he was happy to be in the car with her. Priscilla rubbed his head absently as she went over everything Tyler had said...and everything he hadn't, mainly that he was glad Jake was going home. But what reason could he have had for stealing her dog? It just didn't make sense.

She gripped the seat belt and tugged it away from where it was rubbing on her neck. "I probably should have asked him what Jake was tied to the post with."

Gail shot her a sideways glance. "Who?"

"Tyler. I should have asked if it was rope or cable or something else. That might have provided a clue as to who found him."

Priscilla frowned. It may have even pointed toward Tyler if he wasn't telling the truth, and the rope he said was used on Jake was something the vet's office kept in stock.

Gail quirked an eyebrow. "A clue, huh? You know, not everything that happens on this island is a mystery to be solved."

"Maybe not." Priscilla laughed and relaxed against the seat. "Well, I guess I'll never know for sure what happened, but we're going home now. That's all that matters, right, Jake?" She reached over the seat and gave him a tickle between the ears.

By the time they reached the state highway, Priscilla felt a grumbling growing in her belly. She motioned toward the clock in the dash. "It's almost eleven thirty. I was too worked up to eat breakfast this morning. Wanna pick up some lunch on our way to the cottage? My treat. It'll be my way of saying thank you for all your help and for offering to drive me to the animal shelter."

Gail nodded eagerly. "That's so sweet. I would love that."

"Okay." She thought a moment. "What about some pizza? We could swing into Oak Bluffs and pick up one of those mashed potato pizzas from Offshore Ale."

"Oh my goodness, I love those things. That sounds perfect."

Priscilla pulled her phone from her purse. "I'll give them a call. By the time we get there, they should have it just about ready."

The restaurant was busy when they arrived—another reminder of the upcoming festivities in Edgartown. They ended up having to wait almost fifteen minutes before their order was ready, but Priscilla didn't mind. Now that she had Jake back, nothing else mattered.

She climbed into the car and rested the pizza box on her lap. Jake laid his paws over the back of the seat, and his gaze latched onto the box.

"Forget it, Jake. I may be glad to have you back, but there's no way I'm giving you a slice of this pizza until we get home."

When Jake rested his head on his paws sadly, Gail burst into laughter. "That crazy dog. You've got your hands full with him, Priscilla. No doubt." She took a deep whiff and then patted her stomach. "Can't say I blame him, though. That bacon and cheese smells heavenly. Let's hurry back to the cottage so we can eat it while it's hot."

She pulled onto the street and turned for Misty Harbor. A short while later, they eased into Priscilla's driveway. Gail shut off the engine and swiveled on the seat for Jake's leash. "You've got the pizza. I'll take Jake."

"Okay. Thank you, Gai—"

That was as far as Priscilla got. She grabbed Gail's arm as a tall figure clad in a dark overcoat and wearing a black wool cap barreled from her house.

"Gail, look!"

Both women froze, but Jake began barking furiously and clawing at the passenger side window. The person scuttled across the yard toward a beat-up midsize car parked alongside the road.

"Blue car," Priscilla said, patting Gail's arm frantically. "Remember that. Can you read the license plate?"

"It's too far," Gail said, pressing her hand to her chest in fright.

A second later, the person jumped into the car and drove out of sight.

## CHAPTER SEVEN

Gail blew out a breath and turned widened eyes toward Priscilla. "Who in the world was that?"

"I don't know, but I intend to find out." Balancing the pizza box in one hand, Priscilla scrambled from the car, and then paused and ducked her head back inside. "Bring Jake. I'm going to take a look around."

"Are you sure you should—?"

Before she could finish the sentence, Priscilla had slammed the door shut and started cautiously up the walk. From what she could see, the cottage looked relatively peaceful. There were no broken windows, no door hanging from its hinges. She reached for the knob. The front door swung open with just the slightest turn. Had she left it unlocked? She and Gail had been in such a hurry to get to the vet when they left. She hated to admit it was possible.

Inside the house, everything looked just as she had left it. Their coffee cups still sat on the table, Gail's directory open next to them, and Priscilla's list and pencil nearby. Sucking in a breath, Priscilla set the pizza box on the counter and then crossed to the flour bin and lifted the lid. Nothing looked disturbed. She poked around until she dug out the leather pouch filled with stones. It was intact.

But the suitcase? She shoved the pouch back into the bin and hurried to the living room where she had left it. The suitcase still lay open, but someone had obviously been digging through it. The contents were strewn on the floor in haphazard fashion.

"Priscilla?"

"In here."

She waited until Gail poked her head cautiously inside. "Everything okay in here?"

"Nothing seems to be missing." Priscilla brushed her hands together, creating a puff of white powder.

Gail waved her hand in front of her face with a grimace. "What is all that?"

"Flour," Priscilla said with a laugh. "I'll explain later."

Suddenly it occurred to her why Tyler might have wanted to steal her dog. She froze and backtracked in her mind, counting the minutes since she'd left the vet's office until they arrived home.

"Gail, can you keep an eye on Jake for just a moment longer?" she said, urgency in her words.

The smile faded from Gail's face. She drew herself up and threw a sharp glance around the room. "Of course. Is something wrong?"

"Everything's fine, I think, but I need to make a phone call."

At Gail's nod, Priscilla returned to the kitchen and grabbed her phone. She still had the number to the vet's office in her recent call list, so she hit redial and waited for someone to pick up.

"Animal Health Care Associates."

Priscilla recognized the voice immediately. "Hi, is this Mary?"

"Yes, it is."

"This is Priscilla Grant."

"Hi, Ms. Grant." Mary's voice took on a worried edge. "Is everything okay with Jake?"

"Everything's fine, but I thought of one other question I'd like to ask Tyler. Is he available?"

"No, I'm sorry, he's not. He got a phone call right after you left and had to hurry home."

Priscilla gripped the phone tightly. *Right* after I left?"

"Uh-huh. I assumed it was some kind of personal emergency. We've been pretty slow this morning, so I let him go." She paused, and Priscilla heard her take in a long breath. "Ms. Grant, is everything all right?"

"Everything's fine, Mary, but by any chance, did you happen to see what kind of rope Jake was tied to the pole with? Was there anything special about it in any way?"

Confusion colored Mary's voice as she stumbled to respond. "Why, no . . . I mean . . . it was just a rope—the plain old white kind that my mother used as a clothesline. I threw it away just a little bit ago. Do you want it?"

Doubting she'd get any clues from a piece of plain rope that could be purchased at any hardware store, Priscilla declined. "That's all right. Thank you, anyway, Mary. Goodbye."

Gail entered the kitchen with Jake trotting at her heels. "What was that all about?"

Priscilla let out a troubled sigh. "Gail, how tall would you say the person leaving the house was?"

She shrugged. "I don't know. Five-ten, maybe, or six foot. It was hard to tell with the distance between us. Why?"

"And how tall do you think Tyler from the vet's office was?"

Gail's mouth pulled into a troubled frown. "Priscilla, there's no way it could have been him. We just left there."

"Actually, there is." She pointed to the phone. "I just got done talking to Mary. She said Tyler left right after we did. He claimed he got a call from home and had to leave."

Gail's eyes widened. "And we stopped for pizza."

"Exactly, so he would have had plenty of time to get here before us."

Gail raised her hands in a confused shrug. "But how could he know we'd stop somewhere on the way? And why would he do that? He was the one who found Jake."

"Did he? What if he was the one who *took* Jake just so I would get out of the house? But he wasn't fast enough, and we caught him in the act."

"The act of what?"

It had to have been the pouch he was after. The other items from the suitcase were still there. Priscilla crossed to the flour bin and pulled out the pouch. Dumping the contents on the table, she stepped back for Gail to look.

"The act of stealing these," she said, propping her fists on her hips. "I found them last night when Jake kept clawing at the side of the suitcase."

"What in the world?" Gail picked up one of the rocks and held it to her eye. "What do you suppose they are?"

"No idea, but I think I'd better find out," Priscilla said. "It may not have been Tyler, but I think whoever we caught leaving the cottage was after them, specifically."

Gail pondered this a moment and then replaced the rock inside the pouch. "I really don't think it could be him. It doesn't make any sense that he would try to beat us home from the vet, especially since he left after we did. But it can't hurt to investigate a little. Do you want me to see what I can find out about him?"

"Would you?" Priscilla touched her finger to her lip as another thought occurred. "Oh, and did you get the text I sent you yesterday with the photos from the suitcase?"

Gail patted her pocket. "Yep. Joan, Trudy, and I will start asking around town to see if anyone knows them."

"Thank you."

"No problem." Gail looked at her watch. "I'd probably better get going. It's almost one, and I need to check on Pop."

"What about our lunch?" Priscilla motioned toward the pizza box. "Would you like me to package some up for the two of you?"

"Would you mind?"

"Of course not."

Priscilla quickly prepared a take-home bag, thanked Gail again for her help with Jake, and then waved as Gail backed out of the driveway and turned toward home. Her own stomach rumbling, Priscilla plucked a bacon crumble off the top of the pizza and chased it with a glass of cold water from the tap. At her feet, Jake sat watching, his soulful eyes clearly prompting her to remember her promise in the car.

"I know, I know. C'mon, I'll get you a slice," Priscilla said, smiling. She put a piece of the pizza on a plate and set it on the floor for him—a rare treat that Jake gobbled down in less time than it took her wash her hands. Unable to resist his pleading gaze, she tore off a piece of plain crust and set it on the plate.

While he ate, she pushed her arms into the sleeves of her coat. "All right, be good, Jake. I'll be back in a little bit."

He didn't even lift his head as she opened the door and headed for the backyard.

Outside, everything looked perfectly normal. Patches of snow still dotted the lawn like bits of cotton, but even those were rapidly disappearing beneath the rays of sun peeking out from the clouds. Priscilla wandered toward the edge of the yard where she had spotted Jake yesterday, enthralled by something she could not see. The ground here was soft, the grass matted by mud and melting snow, but just a tiny way off, where the ground was firmer, she thought she could clearly make out the impression of a shoe print.

Priscilla inched closer, careful not to disturb the ground and damage the impression. Once she was close, she lowered into a crouch for a closer look. It was indeed a footprint. The impression went deep, like it had been left by a foot with a bit of weight above it. The *kind* of shoe that had made it was also clearly visible—a work boot with a rounded toe.

Removing her phone from her pocket, Priscilla snapped a quick picture and then took off her own shoe and laid it next to the footprint for reference.

Balancing on one foot and one very chilly toe from her other foot, she managed to take several pictures from a variety of angles. Finally, she put her shoe back on and then took one last picture with her finger in the footprint to show the depth. Satisfied that she'd captured the footprint from every possible angle, she shoved her phone back into her pocket and stood.

Her stomach rumbled, reminding her that she had yet to eat her own piece of pizza. But she still had to get someone out to take a look at the invisible fence. Her rumbling stomach won out. She headed inside.

While she munched on her pizza, Priscilla printed out copies of the pictures she'd taken of the footprint. Obviously, one footprint wasn't much of a clue, especially since the tour bus meant dozens of visitors every week. She could hear the police chief's voice echoing skeptically inside her head, asking if she knew how many people went by her cottage and the likelihood of matching one footprint out of so many. Still . . .

Once she finished with lunch, Priscilla stored the rest of the pizza in the refrigerator and tidied the kitchen before heading to the file cabinet for the name of the company she had hired to install the invisible fence. She called them and found out that it would be a couple of days before they could send someone out to check on it, but that only meant that she would have to keep Jake on a leash when she took him outside.

"Jake, ready for your walk?"

Hearing his name, he let out a soft whine and scrambled to his feet, his nails making scuffling noises on the wood floor.

"All right then, let's go." She took his leash off the hook, snapped it onto his collar, and then led him outside.

The days were definitely cold now, but several brave souls still wandered the shoreline, picking up shells or taking pictures. Priscilla kept up a brisk pace, but Jake still tugged every now and then, pulling on her arm as he darted off to chase a seagull, or explore some tuft of willowy sea grass.

Priscilla headed farther down the beach, anxious to let Jake have more of the leash so he could work off some of his energy. Even from this distance, it was easy to keep one eye on the cottage, sitting high on the bluff the way it did, although really, what would she do if she saw someone skulking around?

"Mrs. Grant?"

Priscilla turned and lifted her hand to shade her eyes as she heard her name called. A large figure in a bright orange coat approached, but with the sun at his back, it took her some time before she could make out the features of Robert Peterson.

She dropped her hand from her eyes and stuck it out to shake his. "Mr. Peterson, how nice to see you."

He shook her hand and with his other hand waved dismissively. "Call me Robert, please. I stopped being Mr. Peterson when I retired from the post office." He let go of her hand and motioned toward the beach. "Nice day."

"Yes." Jake circled her legs, and Priscilla switched the leash to her other hand, suddenly glad for a dog's presence, even one as mild-mannered as Jake. "Just taking my dog for a walk."

"He's a cute fella." He tipped his head toward Jake. "Do you mind?"

"Not at all." Priscilla gripped the leash tightly. "Here, Jake."

To her surprise, he ambled immediately to her side and sat obediently by her feet. Robert bent toward him, but Jake gave a warning growl that Robert heeded with upraised hands.

He retreated a step. "Oops. Maybe not."

"Jake!" Priscilla scolded. Heat warmed her cheeks. "I'm so sorry, Robert. I don't know what's gotten into him."

Except for the low growl, Jake seemed content to remain at her feet.

"It's all right. He's a good dog," Robert said, "and obviously protective of you. What kind of breed is he?"

"Uh...I'm really not sure," she said. She shuffled her feet against the hardened sand. "A mixed breed, I suppose. I've only had him a little while."

He motioned toward the beach. "You live around here?"

Priscilla pointed back up the coast, unsettled by his questions yet not sure why. "Just over there."

"The lighthouse on Misty Harbor? I know that place."

The wind whipped up and tossed her hair into her eyes. She smoothed it back behind her ear. "You've heard of it?"

He nodded. "I've driven by it several times. Must be a pretty view from up there. Have you lived there long?"

"Not really. It was my aunt's place. She left it to me when she passed away."

His face fell. "Oh, I'm sorry to hear that."

"Thank you."

"Still, it's a beautiful spot."

"Jake and I enjoy it," she said, forcing a smile. Though she had no reason to be, she was anxious to get back to the cottage and enjoy the safety of its four walls. She gave a tug on the leash. "Well, we'd better be going. It was nice seeing you again, Robert."

"You too. Bye, Jake. Maybe next time, we can be friends."

He stood watching with his hands in his pockets as they made their way back toward the cottage. Priscilla got the distinct impression that he'd been there for some time. Watching.

She shivered as she let herself into the house. Surely it had to be her heightened senses after seeing someone lurking near the house that had made her so skittish. Or maybe it was just the fact that Jake had been made nervous by him. She'd heard dogs were good judges of character.

"Well? What about it, boy?" She crouched to give Jake a good rub. "Do you think Robert Peterson is a nice guy?"

In response, he ran to the living room and came back with one of his chew toys.

Priscilla laughed as she took off her coat and hung it next to Jake's leash. Prying the toy from his mouth, she tossed it for him, initiating a game of fetch that would likely last until her arm gave out.

While Jake hunted for his toy, Priscilla crossed to the large picture window that overlooked the sea. She had a good vantage of the beach from here, a clear line of sight all the way down to the white-capped water. Seagulls circled the shore, their cries muted by the glass, but in her mind, she heard them clearly. People still dotted the shore, but Robert Peterson was gone, his bright orange coat no longer visible. She wished she could've seen the direction he'd taken. It might have eased her discomfort at having bumped into him so unexpectedly.

Suddenly she knew why her meeting with Robert had made her so nervous. Priscilla gripped the wooden sill, angered with herself for not having realized it sooner. It wasn't the conversation that bothered her—that was nothing more than benign small talk.

It was his shoes that had sparked the unease, even though she'd only managed a glimpse when he bent to pet Jake. Robert had been wearing work boots. And they had a rounded toe.

## CHAPTER EIGHT

Priscilla spent all the rest of that evening and part of the next morning pondering what she'd found and worrying about what to make of it. While a pair of work boots wasn't much to go on, work boots outside her house was a little more interesting, and work boots outside her house on a strange man with a distinctive tattoo really made her think.

She waited until she was sure Gail was awake before she called and filled her in.

"Lots of men wear work boots, Priscilla," Gail said groggily. "It really isn't all that unusual that Robert Peterson was wearing them, especially given that he used to work at the post office. They give your feet a lot of support. I bet he wore them all the time."

Gail's voice was skeptical when Priscilla wanted it to be convinced. She clutched the phone to her ear and paced the length of her kitchen and back, her steps quickening with her agitation.

"You're right, I know, but don't you think it's unusual that he would be right here, right outside my cottage so soon after everything that happened with Jake? And don't forget the person we saw leaving after we got back from picking him up at the vet."

"I haven't forgotten, but how can we be certain the two people are the same size?" Gail asked. "Oh, hold on a sec." A TV droned in the background, and her voice became muffled as she covered the mouthpiece. "Hey, Pop, could you turn that down a tad?" The noise faded, and Gail returned. "Sorry about that. I just came into the kitchen to grab a cup of coffee, and Pop has the morning news on."

"That's okay."

"Anyway, about the guy. You can't be sure at all that it was him, can you?"

"Well, it was kind of hard to tell with Robert wearing a heavy coat, and the person outside the cottage was pretty far away," Priscilla admitted. She gave a low groan. "You're right. We couldn't pick him out of a lineup, could we?"

She carried her empty coffee cup to the sink. After drinking two cups while she waited to call Gail, she knew she'd have a case of the jitters later unless she ate something. She plunked a couple slices of bread into the toaster and pushed the On button, then turned and rested her back against the counter. "Anyway, I'm going to keep my eye on him and see if he does anything else that might be suspicious."

"That's probably not a bad idea. I wish I could help on that front. Unfortunately, I don't even know what he looks like."

"That's all right." Unable to remain still, Priscilla pushed off the sink and resumed pacing. "What about the pictures? Any luck with them?"

"Not at all. Sorry, gal. Nobody I talked to had ever seen those people before."

"Hmm. I wonder if Trudy or Joan had any luck."

"Do you want me to ask them? Joan will probably be calling soon. She always checks in about this time."

Priscilla glanced at the clock above the refrigerator. She and Gail had been talking for a while, and she still had to wash and dress. She shook her head. "No, I think I'm going to ask them to stop by. I want their opinion on those rocks I found in the suitcase. Maybe they can shed some light on what they are." She paused. "What about you? Are you busy later today?"

"No, I'm off today. Why?"

"Do you think you could come over for a little bit?"

"Of course. What time?"

Priscilla did a quick calculation in her head, then decided to push for later to give herself plenty of time to get organized. "Make it around noon. I'll have lunch ready." She crossed to the refrigerator, checked the contents, and then closed the door. "Could you pick up some lemons on your way over? I'm out."

"No problem. Anything else?"

"Nope. That'll do."

"Okay. See you then."

Gail disconnected, and Priscilla called Joan and Trudy before sitting down to eat her toast and then heading to the bathroom to freshen up. Once she was dressed, she returned to the kitchen and set about pulling all the ingredients for a grilled chicken salad out of her refrigerator. It wasn't hard, since she'd purchased a roasted chicken at the market the other day and still had plenty left over to add to the salad. With some boiled eggs and freshly shredded cheddar, she knew it would make for a tasty and satisfying meal.

While she worked, she thought about Gerald. It had been some time since they'd talked. If he'd discovered anything new about the knife they'd found inside the suitcase, she knew he'd call, but she still determined to check with him after her cousins left. He might even be able to tell her something about Robert's eagle tattoo. She added it to the list of questions she would ask the next time they spoke.

Done with the staples for the salad, Priscilla added some chopped pecans and threw in a handful of dried cranberries as a garnish. The finishing touch was a sweet yet tangy citrus dressing she'd purchased at a specialty store during her last visit to Boston. For a brief moment, she wished she'd also thought to pick up some mandarin oranges, then decided the salad was substantial enough without packing on more.

She stood back to examine her work and smiled. "There, that looks festive."

She set the bowl and dressing in the center of the table, then laid out four place settings. When that was done, she put a kettle on to boil for brewed iced tea. The bags had just finished steeping when her doorbell rang.

She went to answer it, not surprised that Joan had arrived first. She had sounded the most eager to hear what Priscilla had learned when she called, and promised to head right out the door when they hung up. In her hands was a box from Candy's bakery, and she held it high with a smile.

"I brought dessert."

Priscilla pushed the door wide and let her pass. "Oh, yum. What did you bring?" Before Joan could answer, she held up her hand. "You know what? It doesn't matter. Anything from Candy's is good."

Joan laughed and gave the box a gentle shake. "That's true, but some cookies are better than others."

Priscilla immediately felt her mouth water. "Chocolate chip?"

"Your favorite."

"You're a jewel." Priscilla motioned toward the kitchen. "C'mon. I have some iced tea ready. I'll get you a glass, unless you want to wait until Gail comes with the lemons."

"No lemon for me. Plain tea is fine. Is that a hint of ginger I smell?"

"Uh-huh. I found a store in Boston that specializes in organic teas. This one is ginger, but I have a hibiscus blend I'm dying to try."

"Well, they both sound heavenly. I'll have to get the name of the store from you later so I can order more of that pumpkin spice chai the boys got me for Christmas last year. I'm completely out."

"Pumpkin spice chai? Oh my, I bet that would be delicious this time of year."

"Uh-huh. I drink it hot with just a little bit of milk and sugar." Joan patted her stomach and smiled.

Priscilla laughed as she led Joan to the kitchen. A short time later, Gail joined them, and Trudy arrived just behind her. She blew into the kitchen on a cloud of energy and expensive perfume, pausing to wrap all three of them in a hug before plopping into a chair at the table across from her cousins.

"Sorry I'm late. Wouldn't you know—I had a flat tire. Came completely out of nowhere. The car was fine when I parked it yesterday afternoon." She shook her head in disgust. "I ended up having to trade vehicles with Dan so he could take mine into the shop to get it fixed. I hope I didn't miss anything."

Joan handed her a glass of iced tea, the sides dripping with condensation, and a plate of the lemon wedges that Gail had sliced after she arrived. "Not yet, but you're lucky I saved a cookie for you." She pointed to the box on the counter.

"Cookies from Candy's? That is a treat." Trudy squeezed a bit of lemon into her tea, then brought the glass up to her nose. "Do I smell ginger?"

"Yes, and it's delicious," Joan said.

Trudy took a small sip and then widened her eyes. "Yummy. Where did you get it?"

Priscilla described the store. While she talked, Trudy nodded.

"I know that place. Great little store. I get my turmeric tea there. And they have a great little strawberry blend that's to die for. But enough about tea." She twisted in her chair to look around the kitchen. "So? What's this about a hidden pocket in the suitcase? And where is the suitcase, by the way? I still haven't seen it."

Priscilla picked up the salad bowl and passed it to Gail, along with a basket of warm breadsticks. "I put it under the bed in the guest room. After our little visit yesterday, I thought that would be safer than leaving it out."

Trudy set down her glass and reached for another lemon to squeeze into her tea. "What visit?"

Gail took a healthy serving of salad and passed the bowl to Joan. "Priscilla and I caught someone running out of her house yesterday."

Joan went still, the salad tongs frozen in her hand and her eyes large. "What?"

"Well, not exactly *caught*," Priscilla said quickly. "The person was running away as we pulled up."

"Oh, Priscilla, how frightening. Did you call the police?" Joan set the salad bowl down and reached out to grip her hand.

Gail answered before Priscilla could. "And tell them what? They pulled everything out of the suitcase, but nothing was missing."

Joan shook her head firmly. "They still broke into her house. That, in itself, is illegal."

Priscilla nibbled nervously on the tip of her fingernail. "Um..." Her hesitation instantly drew her cousins' curious stares. She dropped her gaze and fiddled with her breadstick. "That may not be exactly true. I mean, they may not have broken in."

"What?" Joan pulled her hand away. "What do you mean?"

Priscilla's cheeks warmed under Joan's look. She took a sip of her iced tea. "The truth is I may have left my door unlocked because I was in such a hurry to get to the vet to pick up Jake."

Joan still didn't look satisfied with her answer, but she let the subject drop.

Trudy plucked one of the breadsticks from the basket and set it on her plate. "Well then, it's probably a good thing you hid the suitcase, but I want to take a peek at it after we eat. I'm curious what it looks like."

"Me too," Joan admitted. She watched as Gail drizzled dressing over her salad and then put out her hand for the bottle. "Have you seen it yet, Gail?"

Gail nodded and swallowed a bite of her salad. "Priscilla showed it to me the day I came over to help her find Jake."

Trudy's eyes widened, and she stared at Priscilla across the table. "You lost Jake? I thought you said you picked him up from the vet."

"*A* vet...not *his* vet. And I only lost him briefly." Priscilla explained about Jake's disappearance and the steps she and Gail had taken to find him. "And speaking of the vet, do either of you know a young man named Tyler Phillips?"

Joan and Trudy exchanged a glance. "Who?"

"A young man who works at the vet's office, the one on the south side of the island."

"Animal Health Care Associates," Gail added around a mouthful of salad.

"Maybe." Joan set down her glass. "How old is he? Did he go to school here on the island?"

Priscilla paused to think. "He's in his mid-twenties, or so, I guess. Gail?"

She nodded. "About that." She plucked a crouton from her salad and popped it into her mouth.

Joan shook her head. "I wouldn't know him. Both of my boys are older than that."

"Mine too," Trudy said. "Why?"

Priscilla picked through her salad. "No reason. He was just acting a little strange when I went to pick up Jake."

"Well, I'm glad you found him," Joan said kindly.

"Me too." Trudy swallowed a bite of chicken and then pointed at her salad with her fork. "This is delicious, by the way."

"Thank you." Priscilla pressed her napkin to her mouth and stood. "And there are cookies for dessert, thanks to Joan."

She crossed to the counter, picked up the box, and carried it back to the table. When she lifted the lid, all three of her cousins leaned in and took a deep whiff.

"I sure would like to know what Candy adds to her recipe to make her cookies so delicious," Trudy said with a sigh. "Mine never turn out like hers."

Joan's eyebrows rose skeptically, but her twitching lips implied mischief. "You cook?"

Trudy sniffed and removed one of the cookies from the box. "I have been known to whip up a tasty dinner on occasion. I have an outstanding recipe for a very nice cheese soufflé."

They all laughed, and Priscilla refilled their glasses to enjoy with the cookies. Once they were finished with lunch, she went to the guest room and brought out the suitcase for them to examine.

Joan traced one of the long scratches across the surface with her finger. "It looks so old, like something from Mildred's museum."

Trudy fiddled with one of the leather straps. "Isn't this kind of suitcase called a Morgan?"

Priscilla looked at her blankly. "A what?"

"A Morgan." She flipped the suitcase over and pointed to a piece of leather stitched onto the front and embossed with a pair of wings. "Yeah, there it is. I think that's the symbol for the Morgan Motor Company."

Gail stared at her, her eyes rounded with amazement. "How do you know that?" She motioned toward the suitcase. "And why would a motor company logo be stamped on an old piece of luggage?"

"Well, they make cars—very, very expensive cars—but they also make luggage," Trudy explained. "I read about them once in one of those in-flight magazines. You know, the kind you see in the pocket under your tray table."

"Where is this company based?" Priscilla asked. Her interest was in more than a car company. Surely the unusual and expensive luggage could provide a clue as to the owner.

Trudy nibbled her lip, thinking. "Somewhere in England, I think."

"England." Priscilla tapped the edge of the suitcase. "Anybody notice a tourist with an English accent recently?"

"No, but we can certainly add it to the things to be on the lookout for," Gail said. She patted Priscilla's arm. "Show them the other thing."

"What other thing?" Joan and Trudy asked in unison.

Priscilla led them back into the kitchen. They watched in fascination as she pulled the small leather pouch from her flour bin.

"That can't be sanitary," Joan said quietly.

Trudy's face twisted sourly. "What is that, and why did you put it in your flour?"

"For safekeeping," Priscilla said, stifling a laugh at their mutual looks of disgust. She carried the pouch to the sink, gave it a firm shake to dislodge any flour clinging to the sides, and then poured the contents of the pouch into her palm.

All three of her cousins fell silent for a moment, and then Joan looked up curiously. "When did you become a rock collector?"

"I didn't. These were in the suitcase."

Trudy scratched her temple. "I don't get it. Why did you hide them and not the rest of the stuff that was inside?"

Priscilla explained how Jake's curiosity had led to the discovery of the hidden compartment inside the suitcase. "Anyway, I figured if the owner of the suitcase cared enough to hide them, they must be worth something. Hence the flour bin."

Trudy picked up one of the stones and held it up to her eye. "Well, I've seen prettier quartz. Maybe it would look better if you shined it up a little." She turned on the tap and held the stone underneath the stream of water. When she finished, she pinched the stone between her thumb and forefinger and held it high for them to see. "There you go. What'd I tell you?"

A ray of sunlight chose that moment to break free from a thick bank of clouds and shine brightly through the kitchen window. Seeing it sparkle against the stone, Priscilla froze. "Trudy, wait."

"What? It looks much nicer now, right?" She turned her head and a smile materialized on her face. "Hey, do you girls remember doing an art project in school where we took that glue stuff—what was it called?"

"Mod Podge," Gail supplied.

"Yeah, that stuff, and put it on rocks to make them shiny?"

"Trudy?" Priscilla said.

Joan snapped her fingers. "Oh, I remember that stuff. Brett Crane used to spread it all over his palm and let it dry, then peel it off in one big strip."

"Oh, that was so gross!" Gail exclaimed. She gave an exaggerated shiver. "Reminded me of a snake shedding its skin."

"Ladies..." Priscilla looked on helplessly as all three of her cousins broke into giggles recalling a boy and his experiments with craft glue.

Gail pointed at the rock Trudy held and nodded appreciatively. "Wow, that rock really does look nicer."

"*Much* nicer," Priscilla said, cutting in before they could launch into another bout of reminiscing. She took the stone carefully from Trudy's hand and brought it closer to the window. "Look."

Gail's gaze bounced from Trudy, to Priscilla, to Joan. "What are we looking at?"

"That is amazing," Joan said, reaching out with the tip of her finger to touch the stone. Her mouth dropped open, and she turned to gape at Priscilla. "Surely, you don't think...are you thinking what I think you're thinking?"

"Aren't you?" Priscilla looked at Trudy. "Well?"

Trudy's eyes slowly widened. "It could be. I mean...that would explain why they were hidden inside the suitcase."

Gail crossed her arms and glared menacingly at the three of them. "Would somebody please tell me what is going on?"

Priscilla glanced down at the rock in her hand. It *had* to be. It was the only possible answer to the question of why they were hidden and why someone would go to such great lengths to get them back.

She set the rock in Gail's hand. "Look closer. These aren't just rocks, Gail."

Consternation carved deep furrows in Gail's brow. "Well, if they're not rocks, then what are they?"

Priscilla laid one last, lingering look on the stone. She could be wrong, but somehow, she didn't think so. She lifted her head and squared her chin firmly. "If my hunch is right, you're holding an uncut diamond."

## CHAPTER NINE

An uncut diamond." Gail snorted and plucked another stone from Priscilla's hand, then held them up, one to each eye. "That's impossible. These are just some kind of quartz or maybe crystal or . . ."

Her words faded as she stared, mesmerized at the rocks in her hand. Slowly her hands lowered and her mouth formed an amazed O.

"Diamonds? B-but how can that be?" she stammered.

"Look at the size of the largest one," Joan whispered. Her voice quavered a bit. She swallowed and pointed with shaking fingers. "That thing is almost as large as a silver dollar."

"Like the Hope Diamond," Gail whispered back. Priscilla looked at her, and Gail stuck out her lip in a pout. "What? I saw pictures of it once in a book I borrowed from the library."

Trudy whistled, startling them all. Seeing them stare, she shrugged in apology. "Sorry, but do you ladies know what something like that would be worth?"

"No. Do you?" Priscilla asked. Trudy was full of information, so it wouldn't surprise her if she did, in fact, know something about uncut diamonds.

Trudy shook her head, sending her earrings into motion, and put up her hands. "I have no idea. I was asking."

Gail rolled her eyes and handed the stones back to Priscilla. "Here. You'd better put these back in the flour bin along with the rest of those things. If you're right, then I don't want to be the one responsible for losing any of them."

"Me either." Priscilla dropped the stones back into the pouch and shoved it deep inside the flour bin, then dusted off her hands. "All right, so now what? How do we find out what those things are worth?"

"Internet?" Joan said. "You can find just about anything online nowadays."

"Good thinking. Okay. I'll go get my laptop."

Priscilla got her laptop from the living room and rejoined her cousins in the kitchen. She sat down at the table, and all three ladies slid their chairs closer to peer over her shoulder.

Sucking in a breath, Priscilla typed, "How much are uncut diamonds worth?" Soon several images popped up, many of which did indeed look similar to the stones in her flour bin. Underneath the pictures was a list of links. Priscilla scanned the first few, clicked one that looked reputable, and frowned.

"That's it?" Gail said, leaning away from the computer. "A couple thousand dollars per carat? That means that whole pouch would only be worth...what? A hundred thousand dollars or so? Don't get me wrong, that's a lot of money, but I thought it would be more."

"Well it's certainly not pocket change," Joan said. "Think what you could do with even half that."

Gail pointed to the computer. "Do you think you could find out if anyone has put out a reward for a missing suitcase? I mean, even if the stones aren't as valuable as we thought, whoever lost them would still want them back."

"A reward. That's a good idea. I'll check," Priscilla said. Several minutes later, no amount of keyword searches turned up any information of a reward originating anywhere on the island. She expanded the search to Boston and several other nearby cities. Finally she increased the search area to all of Massachusetts and added Rhode Island, Connecticut, and New Hampshire for good measure. Still, she pulled up nothing.

She sat back with a frustrated sigh.

Joan rubbed her chin thoughtfully, a puzzled frown tugging at her lips. "I don't get it. Why wouldn't the owner of the suitcase at least try to get their stuff back?"

"Maybe it isn't their stuff," Trudy said, arching an eyebrow.

"You mean, the stones could be stolen," Priscilla said.

"It would make sense." Gail touched the lid of the suitcase. "I wonder if this is stolen too?"

"It's possible." Priscilla reached for her phone.

"Who are you calling?" Joan asked.

"First, I'm going to call the police and find out if they are on the lookout for any stolen gems. And then..." Remembering what Candy had said about the suitcase having been buried on her beach longer than she had first assumed, Priscilla bit her lip. "The newspapers. I'm going to see if anyone has published anything about a reward for a missing suitcase. Or missing gemstones, for that matter."

Worried lines creased Joan's brow. "Can we help? I can call the papers for you, if you'd like."

Priscilla paused, thinking. "Actually, it would be a bigger help if the three of you continued showing those pictures around the island." She closed her laptop and pushed it away.

Gail nodded and reached for her purse. "We'll get right on it. Anything else we can do?"

"I'm not sure. I'll let you know after I find out what I can about the stones."

The three headed out, and Priscilla placed her phone calls. The one to the police station was accomplished quickly, since she'd already stopped by there once to ask about missing luggage. Gabrielle, the officer who manned the front desk, was curious and slightly amused when Priscilla asked about stolen gemstones. She sobered when Priscilla persisted with her questions, and promised to see what she could dig up.

Her calls to the local newspapers were no less futile. No rewards for missing luggage. No reports of stolen gemstones.

Priscilla set down the phone with a sigh. Apparently, whoever owned the suitcase either did not want to report it missing...or was not able to.

She shuddered, thinking that her first hunch about the suitcase's owner had been right and the person had drowned in the frigid waters of the Atlantic. If that were the case, there was a possibility the body would never be found. Obviously, she didn't know this person, but in all likelihood, they had family somewhere, and she could think of nothing more tragic than having someone you love go missing and never knowing what happened to them.

She shook the thought from her head. Gerald didn't have any reports of capsized boats, so for now, she would assume the person had not come forward for some other reason.

Jake whined and laid a paw atop her thigh. She scratched his head and gazed into his soulful eyes. "I know. I have to keep looking, don't I? I have to know what happened...just in case I'm wrong."

He rested his head on her lap and gave a long puppy sigh, as if acknowledging the work ahead.

"You're right." She gave his ears a tickle and then reached for her phone and pushed back her chair. "I'd better get started."

Traffic along Main Street in Vineyard Haven was as congested as Priscilla had ever seen it since moving to the island. She maneuvered her way carefully through the cars lining the side streets, turned onto Beach Road, and finally arrived at the Tisbury Marketplace, though she still had to drive for some time before she found a parking spot. She patted the pocket of her purse as she climbed from her car, anxious to begin showing the photos now that she had arrived. It was long, tedious work, and even after several hours, she'd not had a single person say the people in the photos were familiar.

Disgruntled, Priscilla shoved the photos back into her purse, deciding to head toward the nearest restaurant and fill her grumbling stomach with something delicious—and fattening. There were several restaurants in this part of town, but tired of the crowds, she elected for takeout. Spotting the cheerful blue sign for the Net Result, she swung that way.

"Priscilla!"

Gerald waved to her from across the street. She waved back and stopped to let him catch up.

"I'm glad I caught you." He jerked his thumb toward the door. "Were you getting something to eat?"

"I was about to." She eyed the uniform peeking out from under his heavy Coast Guard coat. "Coming from work?"

His car keys jangled as he shoved them into his pocket. "I took a break to get something to eat. What about you?"

She sighed and made a circling motion with her finger. "I've been wandering around town all afternoon, trying to find someone who might recognize the people in the photos from the suitcase."

"Any luck?"

She frowned, disappointed to have to admit she'd not had any success. "No. How about you? Any luck finding out anything about that knife?"

"Maybe." He signaled toward the restaurant. "I was just about to grab some takeout too. If you're not busy, why don't we order and head back to my office? We can discuss it there."

Priscilla's mood brightened at the prospect of new information. Plus, Gerald was good company, and it would be nice not to have to ponder her problem alone. "Okay. That sounds nice. Thank you, Gerald."

It took some time for their food to be ready. They ordered drinks while they waited, and Priscilla filled him in on everything she had learned since they talked. Gerald seemed especially interested when she told him her suspicions regarding the contents of the pouch.

When their orders were done, Gerald took the takeout bags from the cashier and followed Priscilla outside to her car.

"So, is there any way to know for sure if the stones really are diamonds?" he asked. "What about talking to a jeweler? There are several in Edgartown." He opened Priscilla's door, waited until she was seated inside, and then handed her one of the bags.

"To be honest, I haven't thought that far ahead," Priscilla said, buckling her seat belt. "But you're right, I could ask. I'll have to think about it, because I'm not sure I want to draw that much attention, at least not until I know if the stones are stolen." She gestured to his SUV, parked just a short way down the street from where she sat. "I'll follow you."

The Coast Guard station where Gerald worked never closed. Someone was always there to monitor the radios and computer screens and to watch the radar for oncoming weather. Tonight,

Seeley was on duty. He pushed his glasses higher on his nose as she walked in, followed closely by Gerald.

"Afternoon, Mrs. Grant."

"Good afternoon, Seeley." She stopped by the counter and flashed him a bright smile. He was a pleasant enough fellow, and he always made her feel welcome at the station. She motioned toward a framed photo of a young woman with two small children on his desk. "How's the family?"

"They're doing fine, thanks." He smiled. "My youngest, Jackson, is cutting his first tooth. He's been a little cranky from it, but nowhere near as crabby as my daughter was. At least he's not running a temp, so my wife is still getting a good night's sleep."

"I remember those days," Priscilla said, laughing.

Seeley took the bag Gerald handed to him, and his eyes widened hopefully. "Fried fish from the Net Result?"

"I know it's your favorite," Gerald said.

"Thanks, Cap." Seeley opened the bag and took a deep whiff. "This will make pulling the night shift a lot easier."

Gerald laughed and motioned Priscilla through to his office. "Holler if you need anything, Seels."

Seeley nodded, but his mouth was already full with a bite of fried fish. Times like this were slow at the station, but that wasn't always the case, and Priscilla knew he and the other Coasties were probably accustomed to eating on the run.

She chuckled as she set her bag on Gerald's desk so he could help her with her coat. He draped it carefully over the back of her chair, then waited while she sat. Afterward, he circled to sit opposite her.

"Mind if I ask the blessing?" he said, clasping his hands atop the desk.

"Please do," Priscilla said, bowing her head.

She enjoyed listening to Gerald pray. Besides blessing the food, he prayed for the safety of his men and their families, and even remembered to make special mention of little Jackson, something that displayed a sensitivity and concern she admired. When he finished, she reached for a fry and popped it into her mouth just as Seeley had done.

He smiled. "So? Finish telling me about the stones. Did you call the police?"

"I did." She wagged her finger at him. "And don't bother looking so surprised," she scolded playfully. "I know to ask for help when I need it."

He laughed and held up his hands, then picked up a plastic fork and took a bite of coleslaw. "Okay. So what did they say?"

"Gabrielle promised to do some digging for me, but I'm not holding out much hope. I think if anyone had reported them stolen, she would have heard something."

He shrugged. "Possibly. Well, at least I can tell you a little bit about the knife." He pushed his drink aside and reached into a drawer of his desk. "An old army buddy of mine is really into military artifacts. I sent him a picture of the knife and asked if he could give me a little information on it."

Priscilla wiped her mouth on a napkin. "And?"

"It's a US Marine Raider stiletto. Dates back to World War II. According to my friend, they're pretty rare."

"Really?" Priscilla touched the diamond crisscrossed handle of the stiletto. "I was starting to think it was just a plain old letter opener."

He smiled and took a drink from his cup. "Hardly. Those things are pretty deadly. They have double-edged blades and are apparently ideal for silent killing." Priscilla shuddered, and Gerald grimaced. "Sorry. That was probably too much information."

"It's okay." She pushed the knife away, content to think more on her dinner than what the knife might have been used for. "What else did you learn?"

He picked up the knife and balanced it across his palm. "Well, like I said, they're pretty rare, at least knives in as good a condition as this one. They're made of some kind of alloy that tends to leave the castings brittle. My friend said the only stilettos he's seen are either cracked or have part of the hilt missing."

"Hmm." Priscilla chewed absently on a bite of fish while she examined the scrolling emblem imprinted on the blade near the hilt. It reminded her of something.

Suddenly, she knew what. Her eyes widened, and she swallowed hastily to keep from choking. "Gerald, I saw a tattoo on a man's arm the other day. I meant to ask you about it."

He put down the knife and reached for a piece of fish. "What kind of tattoo?"

Priscilla pointed to the emblem. "It was very similar to this, but it had an eagle on top."

"Eagle, you say?" He nodded. "That would make sense. It's the Marine Corps logo."

"What?"

He put down the food, reached for the computer monitor on his desk, and swiveled it toward her. With just a few keystrokes, he pulled up an image. The insignia depicted an eagle atop a globe, with an anchor and rope behind.

She moved to the edge of her seat excitedly. "That's it. That's the eagle, anyway, which is all I could see of the tattoo. I remember the way the wings were spread out."

He turned the monitor back. "Well, if he had this tattooed on his arm, he was probably in the military, and a Marine."

"Ex-military," Priscilla said. "He told me he had retired from the post office, but he could have been in the Marines before that." She glanced at the knife. Could it be a coincidence that the knife they'd found inside the suitcase was also from the Marines? She didn't think so.

She wiped her mouth hastily with a napkin and stood. "Sorry, Gerald, I need to go. Thank you so much for supper."

He held a fry in his hand and stopped with it halfway to his mouth. "Huh?" He glanced at the remains of her meal. "You haven't finished your food."

"I know, but I need to see Mildred before the museum closes." She grabbed the stiletto and slid it carefully into her purse, then wriggled into her coat.

"Mildred?" He watched her, his face wrinkling with confusion. "What does she have to do with anything?"

Priscilla quickly shoved the rest of her meal into the paper takeout bag and tucked it under her arm. "Thank you so much for checking on the knife for me. I'll fill you in after I talk to Mildred, okay?"

Gerald rose and followed her to the door. He ran his hand over his head, but his eyes twinkled as she hurried past. "You're a hard person to keep up with, Priscilla Grant. Good luck finding... whatever you're looking for."

She paused to give him a genuine smile. "Thank you, Gerald. I mean it. Thanks for your help."

She waved to Seeley on her way outside and then climbed into her car and set the takeout bag on the passenger seat alongside her purse. The clock on her dash read 5:13, which meant Mildred had either just closed or was in the process of it, but the museum wasn't far. Maybe she could catch her before she left.

She was relieved to see Mildred's car when she pulled into the snowy parking lot of the East Shore Historical Museum. Priscilla grabbed her purse and locked her car before hurrying up the sidewalk. Halfway to the entrance, her heel slid on a patch of ice, reminding her that it was better to take care than to fall and risk a broken bone.

A sign on the storm door read Closed for Renovation. Priscilla pulled the door open and poked her head inside. "Mildred?"

The light was still on in the front entryway, but there was no sign of Mildred. Priscilla eased herself in the rest of the way and shut the door.

"Mildred, are you here?"

Soft music drifted down the hall from the direction of the dining room. Priscilla followed it and found Mildred perched atop a stepladder. Her blue overalls were covered in paint, as was her ponytail. She sat with her bottom lip clenched between her teeth, her face scrunched as she concentrated on getting the line of paint alongside the wide strip of crown molding exactly right. Afraid of startling her, Priscilla cleared her throat softly.

Mildred turned. "Oh, hello, Priscilla. I didn't hear you come in."

"Hi, Mildred. I hope I'm not bothering you."

"Not at all." She set her paintbrush aside and eased down the ladder. "I was just about to take a break."

Priscilla pointed at the ladder. "You've been painting all day? I saw your sign on the door."

"Yep. Started early this morning." She propped her hands on her hips and tipped her head to eye her handiwork. "What do you think?"

Priscilla glanced around the room at the sheet-draped furniture. All the pictures had been removed from the walls, and the china boxed and stacked neatly in the hall. Two walls already sported a coat of buttery yellow paint, and Mildred was almost finished with the third.

Priscilla nodded approvingly. "It's looking really good. I'm so sorry to interrupt."

"Not at all. Like I said, I'm ready for a break." Mildred pulled a towel from a pocket of her overalls and wiped some of the paint from her fingers, then circled the mound of furniture to meet her. "What can I do for you?"

Priscilla clutched her purse. "I'd like to show you something, if you have a minute."

"Of course." She motioned toward the kitchen. "Would you like some coffee?"

Mildred kept a Keurig in the kitchen, so Priscilla knew she wouldn't be putting her out if she said yes. She nodded and followed as Mildred led the way.

"I really am sorry about popping in unannounced," Priscilla said while the coffee brewed.

"Not at all. I enjoy your visits." Mildred grabbed both mugs of steaming coffee and carried them to the table. At the center, a silver tray with matching cream and sugar bowls rested. She lifted one of the bowls. "Cream?"

Priscilla nodded and set her purse on the table next to her. While she explained about the suitcase and the contents inside, Mildred spooned a bit of cream and a teaspoon of sugar into their coffees.

"Which is why I'm here," Priscilla finished, taking one of the cups Mildred offered. "Candy suggested that you might be able to tell me something about the knife. I'm hoping she's right."

While she talked, Priscilla removed the knife from her purse and laid it on the table. Mildred's eyes sparkled as she looked at it. "Is that—?"

"A Marine Raider stiletto, circa World War II, according to Gerald O'Bannon."

"Yes. I've heard of these." Mildred picked up the knife carefully. "I'm surprised to see one in such good condition."

"That's what Gerald said." Though she itched to ask questions, Priscilla sipped her coffee quietly while Mildred examined both sides of the knife. When Mildred finished, Priscilla blew out a breath. "What can you tell me about it?"

Mildred set the knife down and reached for her cup. "Well, let's see." She tapped the handle of her cup. Finally, she shook her head. "I'm sorry, Priscilla. There's not a whole lot I can tell you. World War II artifacts are not really my specialty."

"That's all right. Whatever you can share will help," Priscilla said encouragingly. She reached for her own cup but did not drink. She merely held it between her chilled fingers.

"Hmm." Mildred thought for a second and then held up her finger. "Hold on one minute. I think I might have something that can help."

She rose and left the kitchen. When she returned, she held a large book in her hands titled *Semper Fidelis: A Complete History of the US Marine Corps.* She laid it on the table next to the knife.

"Here we go. Let's see what we can find in here." She opened the book and thumbed through the glossary. While there were several pages regarding changes to the Marine Corps uniform and equipment, there was only one small paragraph regarding the stiletto itself. Mildred read the section aloud:

"The US Marine Raider Stiletto was the first knife in United States Marine Corps history to be designed by a US Marine Corps officer, Lieutenant Colonel Clifford H. Shuey. It was officially issued on a selective basis to the Marines, with priority given to elite units such as the Raiders. Its fine design and slender, almost delicate blade made the stiletto a single purpose weapon—dispatching the enemy. The hilt was die cast using a zinc aluminum alloy, which meant the knives could be produced at a lower cost and with minimal use of coveted war materials. Unfortunately, the hilt castings became brittle over time, leaving very few undamaged Raider stilettos still in existence, making them one of the rarest and most expensive knives in the world of military collecting."

Mildred leaned back in her chair. "Well, that is interesting, but I'm not sure it helps you much with your suitcase. What else did you say was inside?"

"Some old photos, a change of clothes—"

"Men's? Or women's?"

"Men's."

Mildred nodded for her to continue.

"There was also a map of the island, which let me know the owner of the suitcase had probably been on the island at some point. There was also a flashlight—oh, and some kind of foreign currency. Gerald thinks the flashlight—"

Mildred laid her hand on Priscilla's arm. "Wait, foreign currency?"

"Uh-huh. Reais from Brazil, euros from France, Italy, and Germany, even some British pounds. Several bills, though I couldn't tell you how much it would translate to in American dollars."

Mildred tallied the items on her fingers. "Money, a flashlight, and a knife? That sounds like the prop list from a Russian spy movie

I just watched on television. I would laugh, but since we still aren't sure where the suitcase came from, I'm not sure it's funny."

"That's not the most interesting thing," Priscilla said and went on to tell Mildred about the leather pouch filled with stones she suspected were uncut diamonds.

When she finished, Mildred drummed her fingers against the table nervously. "This all sounds very strange, Priscilla...and a little dangerous. Are you sure it's safe keeping all this information to yourself? Maybe you should contact the police."

"I have contacted them," Priscilla assured her quickly. "So far, they haven't been able to tell me anything about a missing suitcase or stolen gems, though Gabrielle promised to call me if she stumbled across anything she thought might be interesting." She paused, thinking. "Mildred, do you know a man by the name of Robert Peterson? He said he used to work at the post office."

"Our post office?" Mildred shook her head. "I don't think so. I know just about everyone who ever worked there, and I don't recall a man by that name."

Priscilla bit her lip. Could he have lied? "I could call the post office. It should be easy enough to find out if he's telling the truth or not."

"Well..." Mildred trailed off hesitantly. "Not necessarily. There are several post offices on the island. Maybe he meant one of those. The one in Edgartown is open on Saturday. You could call in the morning and ask."

Priscilla picked up the stiletto. It fit snuggly in her palm, but remembering its primary use, she shivered and slid it into her purse. "That's a very good idea."

Mildred seemed in no hurry to get back to her painting, so Priscilla settled back and listened to her chat about the many faces that had come to and gone from the island over the years. At first, she hung with rapt attention on her friend's words, but then she remembered the knife in her purse and her thoughts wandered elsewhere.

She took another sip from her cup, savoring the full, bold flavor of the coffee as it warmed her tongue. Yes, she would call the post office the moment they opened, and she knew exactly what she would say. And when she hung up, she'd see what she could do about finding Robert Peterson.

## CHAPTER TEN

Priscilla always felt better when she was *doing* something rather than *waiting* for something. So rather than call when she got up early the next morning, she got dressed and drove the short distance into Edgartown so she could speak to the postmaster face-to-face. Not that he, or she, would give her the answers she desired. Just the opposite. They might not be able to tell her anything about the mysterious Robert Peterson, but at least she wouldn't be sitting at home, waiting for someone to call her back.

The post office was located just off Upper Main Street in a small shopping plaza. On one side it was flanked by a bank, and on the other were several small stores, including a pet store with colorful banners advertising pet supplies in the window. Remembering her plan to buy some new toys for Jake, she made a note to return later that afternoon, and maneuvered her car into a parking spot closer to the post office.

White trim framing the windows and door gleamed brightly in the pale morning sun. Not exactly awash in color, but cheerful nonetheless. Priscilla took off her sunglasses and laid them on the dash. So far, Gerald's prediction for the weather turning sour had not come true. She only hoped the same could be said when Christmas in Edgartown began in earnest on Thursday.

Inside the post office, mats covered the polished floors. Priscilla felt her foot slip on the tiles and immediately knew why. She kept to the mats as she made her way to the customer service window. There, a postal worker, a middle-aged woman with blonde streaks in her hair and rings on several of her fingers, bent over a cash drawer, counting out a stack of one-dollar bills.

Priscilla waited until she finished counting. When the woman finally looked up, Priscilla said, "Good morning."

The woman smiled. "Good morning. Thank you so much for your patience. What can I do for you today?"

"Um..."

Priscilla glanced at her name tag. It read T. Pierce. Perhaps calling would have been better. She glanced over her shoulder. Except for a gentleman standing in front of the post office boxes, sorting through his mail, the place was empty.

"This is probably going to sound a little strange," Priscilla began, "but I'm looking for a gentleman named Robert Peterson. I think he may have worked here?"

"Peterson?" T. Pierce shook her head. "How long ago? That name doesn't sound familiar."

"Oh, I'm afraid I don't know the answer to that."

The woman's face scrunched in a frown. "Huh. Well, let me ask Dave. He's the postmaster here." She leaned over the counter with a conspiratorial smile. "Been here a *lot* longer than the rest of us."

"I heard that, Trish," a male voice called from somewhere at the back of the post office.

A man, older than Trish by several years, appeared from behind a tall partition. He was gray-haired, and his belly more than amply filled the starched blue uniform shirt he wore, but his eyes twinkled merrily from behind a pair of thick glasses as he approached the counter and held out his hand. "Dave Adams, at your service."

Priscilla shook his hand and decided instantly that she liked him. He had a firm, no-nonsense grip, and his palm was warm and callused, not smooth like some other types she'd met. "Priscilla Grant."

"Nice to meet you, Ms. Grant."

"Oh, Priscilla, please."

He smiled and tipped his head slightly in deference. "All right. What can I do for you, Priscilla?"

"She's looking for someone named Robert Peterson who may have worked here," Trish said. "Do you remember anyone by that name?"

"He's an older man, maybe in his mid-to late sixties," Priscilla added.

Dave took off his glasses and used one of the earpieces to scratch his balding head. "Peterson? Peterson. No, I'm afraid I don't recall an employee by that name. He retired from *this* office?"

"Maybe not this branch. He said he retired from the post office, and I just assumed it was one of the local branches. I believe he may have been in the military before he retired, if that helps any," she added.

"Oh, that's not uncommon," Dave said, returning his glasses to perch on his nose. "The United States Postal Service has a long history of hiring veterans, reservists, and their families." He said it proudly, as though he'd rehearsed it several times to say in just such a moment. He hitched his thumb toward the woman beside him. "Trish here is retired Army, but I don't hold that against her."

"Ugh. Sailors," Trish said with an exaggerated roll of her eyes. She propped her elbow on the counter and rested her chin in her palm. "They win a few football games—"

"More than a few," Dave interrupted, his laugh making his belly shake.

*Like a bowl full of jelly?* Priscilla couldn't help but make the comparison, considering the rest of his jolly appearance.

Dave sobered after a moment and smiled sheepishly at Priscilla. "Sorry about that. The competition between the Army and the Navy is an ongoing joke around here."

"Not a problem. My husband was a big college football fan," Priscilla said, returning his smile.

Dave hooked his thumbs into the pockets of his trousers and rolled back onto his heels. "Anyway, like I was saying, if this man you're looking for is a veteran, it's very likely that he could have worked for the postal service. His military service would have been treated as prior employment, which is why so many veterans look to the postal service when their time in the military is done."

That information was enlightening but not exactly helpful. Still, grateful they had bothered to speak with her, Priscilla nodded her thanks. "I see. Well, thank you very much for your time."

"No problem. Anything else we can do for you?"

Trish held up a book of Christmas stamps and raised her eyebrows. "Have any Christmas cards you need to send out?"

"All done," Priscilla said, chuckling at their disappointed expressions. "I like to send them out early. Thanks anyway."

She turned to go but then remembered the photos in her purse. She took them out and handed them to Dave. "Actually, there is one last thing. If you don't mind me asking, do any of these individuals look familiar?"

Dave held the photos close to his face. "Not to me."

He handed them to Trish, who also studied them a moment and then shook her head.

"Me either." She handed them back to Priscilla. "They look like passport photos."

"You're the second person to tell me that," she said. "Thank you, anyway." She returned the photos to her purse and then bid them both goodbye.

Though it had only been a few minutes since she went inside, dark clouds had rolled in from the coast and cast a chill over the morning. A strong breeze had also kicked up, forcing the people ducking in and out of stores to lean into the wind to get where they were going. Priscilla wrinkled her nose in disgust. Days like today, she'd have preferred to stay snuggled up under a warm blanket. The one thing that might brighten a gloomy, unprofitable morning…

Priscilla steered her car toward Candy's confectionery, already plotting how a crème horn or chocolatey dessert would dispel her doldrums. Gail's car was in the parking lot, a pleasant surprise that only furthered Priscilla's decision to head inside. She pinched the lapels on her coat closed at the neck, ducked her head against the bitter wind whooshing up from the coast, and headed for the entrance.

It only took her a second to spot Gail. In her cheery red sweater, she was a bright spot in an otherwise dreary morning. Gail set down her coffee mug and waved while Priscilla wriggled out of her coat and hung it on a peg near the door.

"You're out early this morning," she said as Priscilla pulled out a chair and joined her at the table.

"I went by the post office in Edgartown. I was hoping to find some information on Robert Peterson."

Furrows formed on Gail's brow and then quickly cleared. "Oh, the guy you met at the Steamship Authority."

"Yes, that's him."

While Priscilla waited for her coffee and cinnamon roll to be delivered, she explained about Robert's tattoo and how that had led her to the post office. "The postmaster there told me he didn't remember Robert working in Edgartown, but he said it wasn't unusual for veterans to get jobs through the postal service. Robert could have been referring to any number of branches, I suppose."

"A Marine tattoo." Gail puckered her lips. "Seems like too much of a coincidence that the knife you found in the suitcase was issued to the Marines."

"That's exactly what I thought."

Her food arrived, and Priscilla said a brief grace before reaching for the cream and sugar to add to her coffee.

"I don't know, Gail. It's all very odd," she said, her spoon clinking delicately against the sides of her cup.

"I agree." Gail grabbed her fork and pushed a small piece of muffin around on her plate. "What about that young man from the vet's office. What was his name?"

"Tyler?"

"That's him. We can't forget how oddly he was behaving when you started asking him questions."

Priscilla fought a smile as she tapped her spoon dry on the rim of the cup. "We?"

Color tinged Gail's cheeks. "Yes, well, I'm no sleuth, but this mystery definitely has me interested." She set her fork down and folded her arms on the tabletop. "I do have some news to report. I took the photos you gave me to the dentist office where I work."

Priscilla straightened hopefully. "You found someone who recognized them?"

"Just the opposite," Gail said. "Several of the people I work with have lived here all of their lives. How then, is it possible, on an island this size, that no one has ever seen those people before?"

"There is a lot of tourist traffic," Priscilla said uncertainly. "And since the photos were in a suitcase, I would think they belonged to a tourist."

"Not necessarily. It could have been a local returning to the island." Gail's jaw squared stubbornly. "Anyway, I just can't believe it. I mean no one recognized them—local or tourist?" She put up her hands. "All right, all right. Granted, we haven't talked to *everyone*, but I'm really starting to wonder if those people even exist."

Priscilla let those words stew in her brain while she sipped her coffee.

"So what's the plan for this afternoon?" Gail asked. Their waitress appeared and refilled Gail's coffee cup. She doctored it absently and took a sip.

Priscilla glanced at her watch. "Actually, I need to head home soon. I have someone coming by to take a look at the fence."

"Hmm." Gail balanced her mug between her hands. "If I were a gambler, I'd almost be willing to bet he doesn't find anything wrong."

"You might be right," Priscilla said. "In which case, whoever removed the collar from around Jake's neck only wanted to draw me away from the house. And since nothing was missing...I must still be in possession of whatever they were after."

Gail lowered her voice. "The stones?"

"What else?" Priscilla drummed her fingers impatiently on the tabletop. "I've got to find the people in those photos, Gail. Even with you, Joan, and Trudy helping, it just isn't enough."

"What are you thinking?"

Priscilla fell silent a moment. "Christmas in Edgartown starts Thursday, right?"

"Yes. So?"

"So maybe I'll make up a few flyers, like when people have lost a dog. There will be hundreds of people at the events. Maybe I could hand out a few flyers with copies of the photos and my phone number on the bottom. Who knows? Maybe I'll get lucky and find someone who recognizes them."

Gail's head bobbed. "I think that's a good idea. I'd be glad to help."

"Don't you have to work on Thursday?" Priscilla picked up her fork and cut off a piece of her cinnamon roll.

"Uh-uh. I took the day off so I could take Pop to some of the events. The weather's still supposed to be nice, and I figured it might be the only chance we have to get outside. But handing out flyers will be easy. I could even ask Pop to help." Her grin widened. "I bet he'd love getting in on one of your mysteries. If you get them printed out early, I'll swing by the cottage and pick them up."

"I'll work on them tomorrow afternoon," Priscilla said. Having a plan in place chased away the pall that had been cast by her lack of success that morning. She took another bite of her cinnamon roll. Sighing happily, she pushed her plate toward Gail. "You need to try this. It's heavenly."

Gail picked up her fork and grinned. "You don't have to ask me twice."

She *didn't* need to ask twice, Priscilla realized. Whether it was sharing her breakfast or asking for help, she would never have to ask twice when it came to family. They were there for her, just like she was there for them. The knowledge felt good. Really good. Like being part of a team.

*Team Latham.*

She smiled. If for no other reason than that, she'd never regret having made the move to Martha's Vineyard. She picked up her fork and savored another delectable bite of her cinnamon roll. Well, that and Candy Lane's Confectionery. Both were pretty good reasons to move here.

And figuring out what had happened to the owner of the suitcase?

That was yet another reason to stay.

## CHAPTER ELEVEN

Between getting the invisible fence inspected and hunting through the cottage for things to donate to Trudy's fundraiser, Priscilla barely had a moment over the next few days to think about the suitcase. She did manage to squeeze in time to have one of the stones inspected by a reputable jeweler whom Gerald recommended. As she'd suspected, it was an uncut diamond, only slightly more valuable than she'd estimated by searching online. However, remarks the jeweler made about the value increasing significantly once a diamond was cut had sparked a fresh lead in Priscilla's mind—one she was determined to pursue once she'd finished in Edgartown.

She snapped a leash on Jake's collar, climbed out of her car, and headed toward the center of town. If the merry expressions on the faces of people Priscilla passed were anything to judge by, Christmas in Edgartown was in full swing. Brightly colored sweaters and scarves vied with the scarlet poinsettias brimming from flower boxes and barrels on nearly every corner. Twinkling lights rambled over lampposts and doors, boasting of the festive spirit that cloaked the town. But Priscilla didn't need the sights to know the town beckoned for Santa. She could hear it in the excited hum in the air, mingled with the intoxicating scent of evergreen boughs.

She sucked in a breath as she darted into a shallow corner alongside one of the many painted Santa statues on display. She had expected the village to be busy, but nothing could have prepared her for the number of people strolling the streets and ducking in and out of the shops. Because the event was a fund-raiser for various island charities and nonprofits, most of the businesses in Edgartown participated, which meant heavy foot traffic and lots of holiday shopping.

Priscilla looked down at her practical, rubberized boots. Later that evening, Trudy was hosting a kickoff party for the church fund-raiser, but since she would be doing a lot of walking, Priscilla had opted for comfort rather than style. Maybe she'd have time to go home and change before the party began.

Beside her, Jake whined softly. Priscilla tightened her grip on his leash. As she and Gail had suspected, the check of the fence had shown it to be in perfect working order. And that meant she dared not leave Jake alone until she could track down whoever had removed his collar and driven him across the island.

"It's all right, boy," she soothed gently. "We're just going for a little walk."

Once they were moving, Jake seemed to settle down. He even began to enjoy the many children who stopped to give him a pat on the head or tickle him behind the ears. And to Priscilla's delight, Jake also provided her with ample opportunities to show people the photos she'd found in the suitcase, though she had yet to stumble across anyone who could identify them.

"Looks like bringing you with me was a good idea," she said, glancing down at the dog trotting happily by her side. "Although maybe I should have thought about bringing along a water dish."

Priscilla stopped at one of the many tents selling sandwiches and drinks. Next to the counter was a large plastic tub filled with ice and bottles of water. She could easily pour one of them into a cup. "What do you say, Jake? Should we grab something to eat?"

Jake looked up hopefully, and Priscilla chuckled as she led him toward one of the shorter lines. While she waited for her turn, she scanned the crowd for familiar faces. Her cousins would already be here, no doubt, and probably several people from her church.

No more had the thought occurred to her than Priscilla spotted Tracy Buschman. Tracy ran the homeless shelter housed in Faith Fellowship, so it made sense that she would be attending such a large charity fund-raising event.

Priscilla waved cheerfully. Tracy returned her wave and began winding through the crowd toward her, all the while juggling a Styrofoam cup to keep it from sloshing. When she reached her, Tracy pulled Priscilla into a warm hug and then stooped to give Jake a pat.

"Good morning! What are you two doing out and about?"

"Just enjoying the fun." Priscilla gestured around the full tent. "I had no idea there would be so many people. I mean, Candy warned me, but this is incredible."

"Wait until you see the crowd that gathers for the Christmas parade." Tracy gave a lighthearted laugh. "You won't be able to move, but it's all for a good cause, so . . . " She shrugged and took a sip from her cup. "Oh, man, this spiced cider is so good. You need to be sure to try some. We're handing it out at the church booth along with hot chocolate and donuts."

"It smells wonderful," Priscilla agreed. A couple walked by, each with similar scented cups in their hand. "It looks like several people have already sampled some."

Finished with her cider, Tracy tossed her empty cup into a nearby trash can. "Like I said, all for a good cause." She clapped her mittened hands together. "Well, I need to head back to the homeless shelter booth. Stop by if you get a chance. We're giving out informational pamphlets. And these."

She stuck out her wrist and peeled off a brightly colored rubber bracelet. On the inside was printed the name of the church. On the outside were the words, *I was a stranger, and you took me in.*

"These are so neat," Priscilla exclaimed. "I love this idea. What a wonderful way to promote the homeless shelter."

Tracy smiled. "Keep it. I have plenty more."

"Oh, but I wouldn't want—"

Tracy held up her hand. "Think of it as free promotion. You're a walking billboard for the homeless shelter."

Priscilla thought a moment and then gave a nod. "Okay, but speaking of free promotion..." She took out one of the flyers and handed it to Tracy. "I'm looking for the people in these photos. Would you mind taking it back to the booth just in case someone there knows who these people are? Or better yet, maybe you could help me keep an eye out for them, just in case one of them happens to be here at the festival."

"Of course." Tracy eyed the flyer and frowned in confusion. "Are these people related to you?"

"No," Priscilla said, shaking her head. "I found the pictures in a suitcase that washed up on my beach, and I'm trying to find the owner."

"Oh, I see." Tracy studied the flyer once more and then folded it and put it in her pocket. "All right, I'll call you if anyone at the booth recognizes these people, or if I see anything." She bent to give Jake one last pat. "See ya, Jake. Be good, you hear?" Straightening, she gave Priscilla a smile. "Bye, now."

"Thanks, Tracy."

"No problem. Have fun."

"I will." She slid the bracelet over her wrist and held it up for Tracy to see. "Thank you for the bracelet."

"You're welcome," Tracy said with a wave.

By this point, Priscilla and Jake were next in line. She paid for her order and then stepped aside to wait. It was almost noon. The Teddy Bear Suite was opening soon, so the crowds had begun to thin as people made their way toward the Harbor View Hotel for a glimpse of the hundreds of teddy bears dressed in holiday finery.

"Ma'am?"

Priscilla turned to the checkout window.

The woman pushed a tray toward her. "Your order is ready."

"Oh, thank you." She collected her bag and moved to a seat at one of the outdoor tables. Inside the bag was a grilled panini for her and an order of plain breadsticks for Jake. Priscilla said a blessing and then took one out for him. While they enjoyed their food, Priscilla people watched, something she enjoyed more and more. They were nearly finished with their meal when she spotted a familiar orange coat weaving among the people clustered around the tent.

Priscilla squinted for a closer look. Yes, it was Robert Peterson. She scooped up the trash on the table and shoved it into the bag.

"C'mon, Jake." She tossed the bag into a waste container and set off at a brisk pace in the direction Robert had taken. He seemed to be browsing the many displays set up on the sidewalk outside the local businesses, so it didn't take her long to catch up.

"Mr. Peterson?" she called. He turned, his lips pressed in a partial frown. She smiled. "I'm sorry. I mean Robert."

The frown cleared from his face, and he smiled. He put down the book he'd been examining and turned to greet her. "Mrs. Grant, how nice to see you."

"Call me Priscilla, please."

He inclined his head. "Priscilla." His gaze dropped to Jake. "And you brought your dog with you. Are the two of you enjoying the lovely weather?"

This time, Jake didn't growl the way he had when they ran into Robert on the beach. Still, she looped the leash around her hand, just in case Jake got any funny ideas. "Yes. I'm so glad the snow held off. It's my first time attending Christmas in Edgartown."

He smiled and slid his hands into his pockets. "Mine too."

"Oh?" Her ears perked. "I had the impression you were from Martha's Vineyard."

He shook his head. "No, no. I'm just a tourist. I live in Boston, but this is my first time visiting the island. Funny, huh? Locals rarely visit the attractions that draw so many tourists to their home states."

So she had been on the wrong track completely when she visited the post office. And in a city the size of Boston? Locating the exact office where he'd worked would be like finding a needle in a haystack.

She reined in her wandering thoughts and managed a nod. "I suppose that's right. I'm from Kansas, originally, and I never went to any of the Wizard of Oz museums."

He laughed. Not a forced chuckle but a real belly laugh. Priscilla felt herself warming to him. Surely, if this man owned the suitcase with its many mysterious contents, there was a reason he hadn't reported it missing.

He motioned toward Jake. "Mind if I try again with him?"

She drew Jake closer with a small tug to his leash. "Not at all. He loves the attention."

This time, before squatting to pet him, Robert pulled a bag of pretzels from his pocket and held one out to Jake, who sniffed at the pretzel but didn't take it right away. Robert waited patiently until Jake's tail started wagging, then gave him the pretzel and took out another. Then another. Finally, Jake dipped his head into Robert's hand, and his eyes drifted closed.

"There, now, that's a good boy," Robert said, rising. He brushed his hands together and smiled. "He's a sweet dog."

"Thank you. I love him."

"I can see why."

"I hear dogs are really good judges of character," Priscilla said quietly, testing Robert for his response.

He chuckled, and his head bobbed. "You can say that again. When I was in the Marines, I had a German shepherd named Clyde. Boy, that was one smart dog. I always said I didn't trust people who didn't like my dog, but I trusted my dog when he didn't like people."

Priscilla swallowed nervously. "You served in the Marines?"

He nodded proudly and lifted his sleeve, revealing his tattoo. "Twenty years."

She studied the now familiar logo, then looked into his face. "I thought you retired from the post office."

"Oh, I did, but I retired from the military first." He rolled his sleeve down and then braced both hands on his hips. "I signed up right after high school, so I was only forty years old when I left the Corps. I still wanted something to keep me busy, and the post office was friendly toward veterans."

Priscilla nodded. "I understand they hire a lot of former military personnel. So what made you want to join the Marines?"

A smile twitched on Robert's lips. "Oh, you know, just following in the family tradition."

"Your father was a Marine?"

He nodded and stuck out his chest proudly. "He fought in Guam."

"World War II?"

"That's right."

She gulped, then hid the action with a casual roll of her shoulder. "He...um...he wasn't a Raider, by any chance?"

He shook his head. "No. That was the 1st Marine Raider Battalion. Pop was 3rd Marine Division, though I think both units did see action in the Pacific." He tipped his head back, and nostalgia softened the lines of his face. "Pop used to tell me all kinds of stories about the war. I wish now I had written some of them down, you know? So I could pass them on to my grandkids." He chuckled. "Not that they necessarily want to hear them. Unless it's on a video game, kids get bored hearing stories of the old days."

Priscilla quirked an eyebrow. "That's so true. It seems like everyone you pass now either has a cell phone or a tablet in their hand. No one just sits and visits anymore."

"Exactly."

"So what about you? Where did you serve?" Her reason for asking the question was twofold. One, despite herself, she really did like Robert and was interested in what he had to say. Two, Trudy had said the suitcase was made by a British motor company, so if Robert had served overseas...

"Vietnam. I did two tours there before heading stateside." Suddenly, Robert seemed uncomfortable with the conversation. He glanced down at Jake and then back up at her. "Well, I don't mean to keep you."

"Not at all," she said quickly. "I was just about to get some hot cider. Would you care to join me? My church is passing it out, and I hear it's fantastic."

He looked uncertain for a moment, but then a smile spread on his lips. "That would be nice."

Relief filled her. Southeast Asia was certainly some distance from Europe, but it was becoming more and more plausible that the suitcase did belong to him, and she still needed to find out why he hadn't claimed it. But until she knew he hadn't done anything illegal, she needed to tread carefully. She motioned toward the street, and Robert fell in step alongside her and Jake.

"So tell me more about your father," Priscilla said. "How long was he in the Marines?"

"Actually, Pop was injured in the war."

Priscilla slowed her steps. "I'm so sorry to hear that."

"Don't be. That's how he met my mother." His eyes twinkled with mischief. "She was a nurse. Pop said he knew the moment they met she would be his wife. Unfortunately, Mom didn't agree. It only took him three years to convince her."

Priscilla couldn't help but laugh. "Sounds like a woman who knows her own mind."

"She was." He glanced her way. "She died of cancer a couple of years ago."

Her heart lurched. "I'm so sorry, Robert."

His smile was melancholy. "She was ready to join him, I think. Pop died several years earlier. I think she was just tired of living without him."

Priscilla suddenly found herself hoping Robert *wasn't* involved in anything illicit. She liked him. Her dog liked him.

At least, Jake no longer minded him. Surely he couldn't be all that bad.

They arrived at the church booth, and Robert stepped forward to secure them each a cup of cider. When he returned, they made their way to a table. Priscilla settled Jake comfortably at her feet and then took a sip from her cup. The cider, spicy and just a tad tart, trickled over her tongue.

"Mmm, this really is delicious."

Robert's head bobbed as he lowered his own cup. "It certainly is. Reminds me of the wassail my mother always made around the holidays."

"She liked to cook?"

"Oh, yes. She and Pop were older when they had me. In fact, for a long time, they didn't think they would have children at all because of his injury. So to fill her time, Mom learned to cook. And bake. She was a whiz in the kitchen. And when I came along and surprised them both, well, let's just say I never went hungry."

They laughed, until Priscilla's gaze fell to his feet. Once again, he was wearing the solid-looking pair of work boots. Her spine stiffened. Robert's boots were large, but were they the same size as the footprints she'd found outside her cottage?

She stood. "Would you excuse me for a moment, Robert? I'm going to grab us a couple of those doughnuts."

"Of course." He pulled his feet back out of her way. "Sorry. My big feet are always in the way."

"That's all right." She handed him the leash. "Would you mind keeping an eye on Jake?"

"I'd love to." He patted Jake's head. "We'll wait right here, won't we, boy?"

Jake sat up, his tongue lolling out the side of his mouth as he ate up the attention lavished on him by Robert. Priscilla kept her eye on them as she made her way to the counter, where Tracy waited with a smile.

"You made it! Did you try the cider? I had to come back for more."

"I did, and you're right, it's delicious." She pointed to one of the white bakery boxes. "Would you mind if I took a couple of those?"

"Of course not. Help yourself." Tracy glanced over Priscilla's shoulder. "Who's your friend?"

Priscilla picked up a napkin and used it to pluck one of the doughnuts out of the box. "His name is Robert Peterson. I met him a couple days ago. He says it's his first time to visit the island."

Tracy leaned her elbows on the counter. "Well, be sure to invite him to church on Sunday. We'd love to have him."

"Will do," Priscilla said, plucking a second doughnut from the box. She held them high. "Thank you."

"Enjoy."

She walked back to the table, and Robert shifted to make room for her to pass by him. Though she wanted to know, there was no tactful way to ask how big his feet were.

She handed him a doughnut. "Here you are. To go with your cider."

"Thank you very much."

He wrapped his long fingers around the doughnut and then, to her surprise, he bowed his head. When he finished praying, he looked up and took a hefty bite from the doughnut. While he munched, he looked around.

Priscilla took a nibble from her own doughnut. Robert couldn't possibly have stolen the diamonds. What kind of thief prayed before he ate? Still, she needed to ask him if he'd been to the cottage.

The doughnut turned dry in her throat. She washed it down with a drink of her cider, then fiddled nervously with her cup while she framed her question. "So, um, Robert...did I mention that I own the lighthouse over in Misty Harbor?"

He looked at her curiously. "You did, that day we bumped into each other on the beach."

"Right." Now she just looked silly. She tried again. "Did you know I'm trying to turn the ground floor into a museum?"

Interest glimmered in his eyes as he lowered his cup. "Is that so?"

She nodded. "Of Latham family history, and the lighthouse's, of course. I'm hoping to have it ready by next summer. In the meantime, I get a lot of traffic from Teresa Claybrook's tours. You should check into it—that is, if you're interested in learning more about the lighthouse."

His head bobbed. "I'm very interested. I've seen the lighthouse a couple of times, but I've never actually been there. I would love to learn more."

She watched his face carefully as he answered. Either Robert was an uncannily good liar, or he was telling the truth. She tended to believe the latter, and it filled her with a sense of relief. They finished their cider, chatting about the history of the island and the Latham family tree.

Finally, Robert rose from his chair. "I've enjoyed our little visit, Priscilla."

"It was my pleasure, Robert." She held up her finger. "Oh, and I'm supposed to invite you to church on Sunday. If you're still on the island, that is."

To her surprise, Robert's features darkened, and his gaze grew shuttered. "I'm afraid that won't be possible, but thank you so much for the invitation."

"Of course." Priscilla stood with him. "I hope I didn't say something wrong."

"Not at all." He lifted his empty cup. "Thanks again for the cider."

Without another word, he whirled and strode for the trash can, leaving Priscilla more befuddled than ever before. Why had the invitation to attend church suddenly made him appear so uncomfortable?

And what, if anything, did he have to hide?

## CHAPTER TWELVE

Robert's odd behavior troubled Priscilla the rest of the afternoon. He seemed like a nice man, and her instincts had seldom been wrong before. Why then had he acted so suspiciously when he left? Was it just that her invitation to attend church had made him *that* uncomfortable?

She stopped outside one of the stores. Near the door was a large sign touting a Christmas sale. While she hadn't intended to shop, she did still need a gift for Rachel. Perhaps she could just run Jake home and come back before everything closed.

As though he sensed her intent, Jake growled.

"Oh, come now," she said, glancing down at him. "Surely you've got to be ready to go home."

But Jake wasn't looking at her. His attention was fixed on something straight ahead. Priscilla scanned the crowd. Whatever had him so fascinated had to be lurking in the large throng of people waiting outside the Harbor View Hotel.

"C'mon, Jake," she whispered. "Let's go check it out."

For the first time all morning, Jake seemed hesitant to tag along. He resisted the pull of the leash, and twice Priscilla had to coax him to move. Even his fur bristled as she drew him near to the crowd.

"What's wrong with you?" she admonished. Maybe she really would have to take him home soon. He was acting worse than a toddler.

Frustrated, she looked up the street toward where she'd parked her car. It wasn't far, but the amount of traffic would definitely make navigating tricky. She turned that way and had almost decided to go ahead and leave when she spotted another familiar figure—the man from the Steamship Authority who had been asking about her at the Nautilus Cafe.

Jake emitted a low growl.

Priscilla glanced down at him, and then back at the man. Remembering what Robert had said about trusting his dog, Priscilla squared her chin and coaxed Jake forward.

"C'mon, boy. Let's go see what we can find out."

As she neared the man, Priscilla pasted a bright smile on her face. When she got to within a few steps of him, she leaned forward and said gaily, "Good afternoon."

He appeared startled at first. His eyes widened as he caught sight of her, and he even stumbled back a step when he saw Jake.

Priscilla stuck out her hand. "Priscilla Grant. I own the lighthouse over in Misty Harbor. I heard you were asking about it."

He recovered quickly. He shook Priscilla's hand, though he kept one eye firmly fixed on Jake. "Pleasure to meet you, Mrs. Grant. My name is Clark Williams. Yes, I love that old lighthouse. It's really beautiful."

"Nice to meet you too, Mr. Williams. Formally, I mean. We've run into each a couple of times around town."

He narrowed his eyes. "Oh?"

"I saw you at the Steamship Authority last week," she explained.

The confusion cleared from his eyes, and he bobbed his head. "Oh, yes. I was getting some information about the local hotels." He smiled broadly. "It's my first visit to Martha's Vineyard."

As he talked, he drew closer, a move that drew another growl from Jake.

Priscilla pulled him back with the leash. "I'm so sorry. I don't know what's gotten into him. He's not normally so protective," she said.

Clark shook his head and moved away. "It's probably me." He pointed to a small scar on his lip. "I was bitten as a kid and have been terrified of dogs ever since. They seem to pick up on that fear and react unfavorably."

"I'm so sorry."

He shrugged. "No problem. I force myself to be around them as a way of overcoming my fear, but sometimes I think that just makes them dislike me more. Isn't that right, Jake?"

He stretched out his hand as though to pet him. Jake took one sniff of his fingers and then scrambled to press against Priscilla's side.

"I'm so sorry," she said, struggling with the leash. "I'd better get him home. It's been a long day for us both."

Clark slid his hand into his coat pocket and nodded. "I understand."

"Enjoy the rest of your visit," she called breathlessly as Jake pulled her up the street.

He lifted his hand to wave in reply. Priscilla turned her attention to the car and getting Jake safely into the passenger seat. Once inside, he flopped immediately onto the seat, and when she slid in on the other side, he wriggled until his head was on her lap.

"All right," Priscilla said. "If that's not a sign that it's time to go home, I don't know what is."

Still, his behavior troubled her as she drove carefully past the point where Clark waited in line. Could he have been the one who'd stolen Jake and deposited him outside the vet's office?

She drove the rest of the way home slowly, taking extra care as she navigated the snow-covered streets. If she'd had more time, she could've talked a bit longer to Clark about his interest in the lighthouse. Then again, it could have very well just been a casual interest. After all, lots of people who came to the Vineyard took the lighthouse tour. Why then did she have the distinct impression that there was more he hadn't said?

She sighed as she grabbed Jake's leash and exited the car, troubled by something she couldn't quite pinpoint.

Thinking over the day made her mentally weary as well as being physically worn out by all the walking. As she followed Jake up the path leading to the porch, she debated about going out again to shop for Rachel or attend Trudy's party.

She unlocked the door, and Jake scurried past her and made a beeline for his water bowl. Priscilla laid the leash on the table. Maybe she would skip the party at Trudy's. She could just call her and let her know she wouldn't make it, or she could take a nap and see how she felt afterward.

Placing her toe on the heel of her other boot, Priscilla slid out of one and then the other. The floor was cold underfoot and made her long for a hot shower and a warm pair of socks. She looked over at Jake and patted her leg.

"C'mon, Jake. Let's go—"

She froze. He'd called him Jake. Even though she was fairly certain she hadn't said his name, Clark Williams had called her dog Jake.

## CHAPTER THIRTEEN

Jake panted happily as Priscilla crossed over to him and bent down to rub his fur. Sighing, he shifted to lean into her side and threw his head back, exposing his neck and begging her to tickle there. On his collar, his dog tag jingled merrily. Priscilla gently fingered the shiny metal tag.

Clark couldn't have simply read Jake's name on the tag... could he?

She ran her fingers absently through Jake's fur as she thought back over the exchange—the way Clark had moved away from them at first, and then how he'd tried to pet Jake despite his fear of dogs. Dogs were sensitive to a person's emotions—she knew that much just from watching a few of the dog training series on television. It was entirely possible that Jake's reaction had been in direct correlation to Clark's feelings.

Priscilla backed up a few feet, approximately the same distance Clark had stood from Jake, and squinted her eyes. It was a slim chance, but he could have better vision than she did, which meant he *could* have seen Jake's name on the tag. She hissed a breath through her teeth. Like it or not, the only way she was going to get to the bottom of things was with a little more investigating and some good old-fashioned elbow grease.

Her mind made up, Priscilla headed to the bathroom to wash up and change for the party. A good long soak in the tub would give her just the boost she needed, and she intended to make the most of every minute.

In fact, she did feel refreshed and revitalized when she emerged from the bathroom. She gave her hair a quick style with the blow dryer, added a spot of makeup to her eyes, lips, and cheeks, and then pulled her favorite pair of black slacks and a red wool sweater shot through with silver out of the closet. She hesitated a moment as she debated about choosing something a little less flashy, then after deciding the color would bring out the highlights in her hair, she pulled the sweater over her head. Satisfied with her reflection, she grabbed her coat and keys and turned for the door.

"Be good, Jake," she ordered, giving him a pat at the door. "I won't be long, okay?"

Jake hung his head, but Priscilla deftly coaxed the doldrums out of him with his favorite chew toy and a snack before heading to her car.

Just as Priscilla knew it would, Trudy's house sparkled with Christmas cheer. Faint music and laughter drifted on the air. Lights twinkled from the low stone wall in front of the two-story cottage and atop all the windows. On either side of the flagstone walkway, charming Christmas lanterns topped with ivy and red ribbon lit the path. Pine garland framed the door where Priscilla knocked, and when Trudy answered, a ball of cheery mistletoe danced above their heads. Seeing Trudy in her glittering Christmas dress and strappy gold heels, Priscilla was glad she'd worn the red sweater.

"Priscilla! Welcome." Trudy pulled her inside and then wrapped her in a tight embrace. "I'm so glad you could make it. Come inside and help yourself to the goodies. Tilly brought some of those Mexican wedding cookies that she serves over at the Colonial Inn." She dipped her head to Priscilla's ear. "If you ask me, they're the best thing on the table, so be sure to grab some."

"Wedding cookies. Got it."

Trudy straightened and motioned toward an elegant crystal punch bowl. "Oh, and Dan is just now serving the punch, so go ahead and get yourself a glass."

That said, Trudy flitted off to greet her next guest.

The chatter inside the house grew louder as Priscilla slipped out of her coat and eased toward the dining room, where several of Trudy's guests stood congregated around an expansive wooden table laden with every variety of holiday treat or cookie imaginable.

Trudy's husband, Dan, was a kind man with a giant heart and a genuine love for people, even if he didn't always know how to express it. Spying Priscilla, he lifted a glass of punch, then excused himself to wind his way over to her.

"Hey, Priscilla. Glad you could make it." He took her coat and leaned in close as he handed her the glass of punch. "Gerald is over by the hors d'oeuvres, just in case you're interested."

"Dan!" Trudy appeared from nowhere and slapped his arm then looked apologetically at Priscilla and mouthed, *"I'm so sorry."*

Priscilla laughed and shook her head at her cousin's antics. "You two. I'll see you both later."

She lifted the punch in a mock toast and then wandered toward the closest cluster of guests—a group of ladies from Faith Fellowship. Ida Lee Jones was among them, and since Priscilla liked her quiet spirit, she moved over alongside her.

"Hi, Ida."

Ida peered up through her thick bangs. "Hi, Priscilla."

Priscilla looked around but didn't spot Ida's husband. She leaned closer to avoid having to shout. "Is Randy with you?"

Ida shook her head and set her punch down next to a small plate filled with goodies. "He couldn't make it. He wasn't feeling well."

"Oh, I'm sorry to hear that. It's not the flu, I hope?"

"I don't think so. It's probably just a cold. I left him under a blanket with a warm bowl of soup. Hopefully, he'll be feeling better by tomorrow."

"That's good." Priscilla leaned back to admire the elegant reindeer stitched onto the blue sweater Ida was wearing. "What a pretty sweater. Where did you get it?"

Ida was a sweet woman, and she worked hard to make ends meet and very rarely took time for herself. Her cheeks flamed pink at the compliment. "Thank you." She ran her hand over the glittering reindeer. "Randy gave it to me. An early Christmas present."

"Aw, that's so nice." Priscilla moved her punch to her other hand. "How are things at the diner? Staying busy?"

The tension seeped from Ida's shoulders. Her face brightened, and she smiled. "They're picking up now that the festival in

Edgartown is under way. It's a busy time for us, but the tips are always really good this time of year, so I don't mind."

She looked relieved. Priscilla suspected the extra income so close to Christmas would come in handy. She gave Ida's arm a pat. "I'll stop by some time this week and pay you a visit."

Ida's smile warmed Priscilla's heart. Next time she was in Edgartown, she'd have to remember to pick up a gift certificate, something nice that would allow Ida to pamper herself for a change.

Across the room, Hannah Clayborn was waving energetically. Priscilla acknowledged her with a lift of her chin and then glanced back at Ida. "Excuse me. I'll talk with you later, okay?"

Ida nodded and shooed her toward Hannah, whose flushed face showed her exertion in getting Priscilla's attention. Tendrils of hair had escaped her ponytail and now clung to her damp cheeks.

"Oh, Priscilla, I was hoping I would see you. I've been meaning to stop by the lighthouse for ages, but I just haven't gotten around to it." Her hands fluttered upward. "Isn't this a lovely party Trudy is hosting? Her house is just so pretty, like something out of a magazine. Maybe I can get her to give me some ideas for decorating the bait shop. I know, a bait shop isn't exactly magazine material, but she has such a knack for it. I know she could brighten the place up, make it look festive."

"Hello, Hannah." Even if Priscilla had wanted to say more, she wouldn't have been able to squeeze another word in.

Hannah lifted a canapé to her lips and sighed. "Have you tried these?"

"No, I haven't made it that far yet."

"They are just to die for. I think Clara Lopez brought them. At least, that's what Alma told me. Who'd have thought a librarian would be such a good cook?"

"Well, she does have access to all those books," Priscilla said, hiding a smile behind the rim of her cup.

Hannah stared at the canapé as though stunned by Priscilla's revelation. "You're right. I never thought of that." She gave herself a small shake and held her plate toward Priscilla. "You really should try one. In fact..." She pulled the plate away before Priscilla could take one and motioned to her husband Jimmy, signaling that he should bring her more of the dish.

Priscilla held up her hand to stop her. "That's all right, Hannah. I'll make my way over there eventually."

"Are you sure?" She craned her neck, looking for Jimmy.

"I'm sure. Thanks, anyway."

Priscilla started to move away, but Hannah snagged her arm before she got too far.

"Say, hold on a second. I've been meaning to ask you, what is going on with the lighthouse?"

Priscilla tilted her head. "You mean the museum? It's not ready yet. I'm hoping to have everything done by next summer."

Hannah waved dismissively. "No, not the museum. I mean the light." She drew a circle in the air. "It wasn't spinning right or something, right? I noticed a couple of flashes the other night coming from your direction, but the light wasn't as bright as it normally is, and it came at odd times, like something wasn't working properly."

Priscilla thought hard, then shook her head, perplexed. "Honestly, I had no idea anything was wrong, Hannah. I'll have to talk to Gerald about it, I suppose. Thanks for letting me know."

"Oh sure. No problem. Um..." She grinned sheepishly. "I suppose I should also say I went by there last week, just to check on things for myself."

"You did?"

Hannah held out both hands in appeal. "You know me. I'm the cat that ate...no, that's not right." She laid her finger alongside her chin. "Curiosity that killed...oh, bother." She blew out a sigh. "Anyway, I was curious, so I took a drive out that way. I got out and looked around, but I didn't see anything out of place."

Priscilla couldn't help herself. She glanced down at Hannah's shoes. Work at the bait shop could be pretty strenuous, and if Hannah had come by the lighthouse...

Sure enough, Hannah's feet were clad in heavy duty footwear—not work boots, but more of a hiking boot. Still, it was the type that could easily leave behind the sort of footprint Priscilla had discovered the day after Jake disappeared.

She cleared her throat and tried to appear nonchalant. "What day did you come by the lighthouse?"

"Let's see..." Hannah tilted her head and let her gaze drift to the ceiling. "Last week we got a new shipment of bait and supplies on Monday, and I noticed the strange flashes that night. But I didn't go over there right away, because I got busy helping Jimmy."

At the mention of his name, Jimmy appeared with a plate in his hand, piled high with a variety of canapés. "Helping me do what?"

Hannah took the plate from him. "Hey, hon, do you remember what day it was that I told you I was going over to the lighthouse?"

He scratched his temple. "Well, let's see, we got the bait shipment on Monday."

Hannah made a rolling motion with her hand. "Yeah, yeah, I already told her that."

He hunched his shoulders and his face scrunched as he thought. "It could have been Tuesday." He shook his head. "Nope, nope, that was the day I went into town to get the box of screws for the planks that were pulling up on the dock. I guess it must have been Wednesday, right?"

"Wednesday." Hannah nodded. "Yes, that's right. I had to stop by the bank that day too." She peered sidelong at Priscilla. "Why?"

"Oh, just wondering." Priscilla's face warmed under their curious stares. "Listen, Hannah, this is going to sound odd, I know, but would you mind telling me what size shoe you wear?"

Jimmy snorted, then covered it with a hand to his mouth when Hannah glared. Satisfied he was properly chagrined, she glanced down at her feet. "No, I don't mind telling you. I wear a size ten. Why?"

Priscilla forced a light laugh. "It's just...well...I wear a size ten."

She didn't say more and fortunately didn't have to. Hannah laughed too and held up her hand for a high five. "No glass slippers for us gals, huh, Priscilla? We're made of sterner stuff."

Seeing the source of his amusement ended, Jimmy wandered off, a glass of punch clutched in his hand.

Priscilla smiled weakly then glanced over Hannah's shoulder. "Oh, there's Gerald. I think I'll go ask him about the lighthouse right now. Thanks so much for letting me know about the light, Hannah. Enjoy the party."

She extricated herself before Hannah could say more. Whatever had possessed her to ask Hannah about her shoe size? The boot print was much too large for a woman's foot. She circled around the other side of the room to the fireplace where Gerald stood.

For once, he wasn't in his uniform. Instead, he was dressed in a deep green sweater that accentuated his eyes and a pair of khaki pants.

"Well, don't you look festive," she said, smiling.

"Thank you. You too." He offered her a bottle of water as she approached. She exchanged it for her empty punch glass, which he placed on the sideboard alongside several other empty glasses.

"Thank you, Gerald."

He nodded, then glanced over at Hannah and her husband. "What was all that about?"

She unscrewed the cap and took a sip. "You heard?"

"Only the part about asking me about the lighthouse. Something I should know?"

She frowned. "I'm not sure. Hannah said she saw a bunch of strange flashes coming from that direction the other night and wondered if something was wrong with the light."

Gerald crossed his arms and lines of concentration formed on his brow. "What kind of flashes?"

"Irregular. That's why she asked if something was wrong. She said they came at odd moments and weren't as strong as other times."

He frowned and glanced at his watch. "I'm not aware of a problem, but I'll look into it in the morning."

"I appreciate that." Priscilla thought for a second, then set her water down and grabbed a napkin to dry the condensation from her fingers. "Gerald, that flashlight that we found in the suitcase...was that military issue too?"

He shook his head. "It could be, but it's a pretty common brand. You can pick one up at any hardware store."

There was a huge difference between a million candlepower lighthouse and a hardware store flashlight. The idea should have struck her as ridiculous. Still...

"Gerald, how bright—?"

"Ah-ha. There you two are." Trudy swept toward them, a bright smile on her face, and put an arm around each of them. "You two look much too serious for a party. Whatever you're discussing, it can wait." She motioned toward Dan. "We're just about to start a game, and you two can be my stool pigeons—I mean, my volunteers."

Laughter followed her words, and Priscilla shot a resigned glance at Gerald. There was simply no arguing with Trudy when she got an idea fixed in her head.

"You heard her," Dan said, coming near with a pen and a page of blank printer labels in his hands. He made a twirling motion with his finger. "Turn around. I'm going to stick one of these labels on you, write something on it, and you will have to go around the room asking questions about the person whose name is on your back. First one to figure out whose name they have, wins. Easy, right?"

There were several groans and much laughter as everyone tried to figure out Dan's explanation of the rules. In the end, the game turned out to be a great icebreaker and got everyone chatting, just as Trudy had intended. Priscilla enjoyed herself but was sorry that she'd not had more time to question Gerald. Or anyone else.

Finally, she gave in to a good time and let herself enjoy the party. After all, the mystery wasn't going anywhere. She'd have plenty of time to figure it all out tomorrow.

## CHAPTER FOURTEEN

Priscilla's phone woke her. After staying out so late at Trudy's party, she was tempted to roll over and let it ring, but fearing it might be Rachel, she fumbled for it on the nightstand and hit the Answer button.

"Hello?" she croaked.

"Priscilla? It's Gail."

Priscilla rubbed her eyes wearily and looked at the clock. Startled into alertness by the early hour, she gripped the phone tightly. "What's going on? Is everything okay with your dad?"

"He's fine. Everything's fine. I'm so sorry to wake you, but I wanted to be sure and catch you before you headed out for the day."

Priscilla pushed up in the bed, disturbing Jake, who groaned in displeasure, lumbered to his feet, and padded out the door.

Priscilla rubbed her hand over her face. "That's all right. What's up?"

"The Bah Humbug Walking Tour is tonight. I thought it might be a fun way for you to get a glimpse of Christmas on the island before the Lighting of the Lighthouse at eight. Are you interested? My boss gave all of us tickets, but one of the other hygienists already had plans, so she gave me hers. I instantly thought of you."

Priscilla perked up immediately. The lighting of the Edgartown lighthouse was a local Christmas season must-see, but she'd been so wrapped up in finding the owner of the suitcase, she hadn't even given it a thought.

"That's tonight? I forgot all about it."

Gail chuckled. "I thought so, which is why I figured I'd better call you early, before you made other plans. So? Pick you up at four thirty?"

Priscilla shot another glance at the bedside clock and then did some quick mental calculations. After talking with Gerald at the party, she had planned on visiting some of the local hardware stores to see what she could find out about the flashlight, but four thirty would give her plenty of time to accomplish her errands before meeting Gail.

She threw back the covers and swung her feet over the edge of the bed. "Sounds good. Thanks for thinking of me, Gail. I'll see you then."

She shivered as her toes hit the cold floor. She hadn't yet adapted to the frigid temperatures of winter after so many months of summer on the island. Of course, this close to the coast, she was subject to every whipping wind that blew in off the Atlantic.

Wrapping her robe around herself, she made a beeline to the bathroom to wash up and change before heading to the kitchen for a quick bite of breakfast. Once that was done, she cleared the dishes from the sink and made sure Jake had plenty of food and water before making the drive into town with the flashlight from the suitcase tucked safely inside her purse.

Like yesterday, tourist traffic was heavy, even in Vineyard Haven, and it took her some time to weave her way to the nearest hardware store. Though there were many to pick from on the island, Priscilla suspected the owner of the suitcase might have chosen the one closest to where the suitcase had been found. If the flashlight had been purchased on the island at all.

She sighed as she stepped through the automatic doors. Chances were slim that she'd find the exact place where the flashlight had been purchased, but it was at least worth a look. She might even bump into someone who could tell her how strong a flashlight of this type could be since she'd been interrupted when she tried to ask Gerald.

By the third stop, however, having gained little useful information, Priscilla had begun to second-guess her decision.

She skipped the checkout lanes of the fourth store and went directly to the customer service desk. A youngish man with close-cropped hair and a wide smile nodded at her as she approached.

"Good morning. Welcome to Carter's. My name is Joseph. How can I help you?"

"Hi, Joseph." Priscilla introduced herself and then lifted the flashlight from her purse. "By any chance, does this flashlight look familiar?"

His grin widened. "Absolutely. I own two of them myself. That's one of our best-selling tac lights." He pointed. "They're in aisle five. Here, let me show you where we keep them."

He started around the counter, but Priscilla quickly held up her hand to stop him. "No, that's all right. Actually, I'm wondering about this particular flashlight."

Joseph's smile disappeared, replaced by a lifting of his eyebrows. "Is something wrong with it? There's a two-year, money-back guarantee on those flashlights. If it's broken, I'll be happy to issue a replacement."

The earnest young man made it difficult for Priscilla to explain what she needed. She set the flashlight down and shook her head. "Well, as a matter of fact, this one isn't working. It got wet, you see, and the inside is quite corroded, but that's not why—"

"Have you tried putting in new batteries?" He made another sweeping gesture with his hand. "Those are in aisle two. We could try, if you like, but even if that doesn't work, I'm pretty sure the warranty is still good because they're supposed to be fully submersible."

The phone rang, and he excused himself to answer, giving Priscilla time to figure out a new plan of attack. When he hung up, she jumped in before he could launch into another round of praise for the ability of the tac light and its outstanding warranty.

"Listen, Joseph, I really appreciate all the information, but I'm not here to replace this flashlight. I really just need to know what you can tell me about this one in particular."

Uncertainty flickered in his gaze. "Oh, okay. Sure. What do you need to know?"

Finally. Priscilla blew out a breath. "Well, to start with, can you tell me how strong this flashlight is?"

His head bobbed excitedly. "No problem. These are really good lights. The promotional material says it can be seen from two nautical miles away. It's supposed to be, like, twenty times brighter than a normal flashlight."

She rolled the light in her hands. "Twenty times, huh?"

"Yep. Plus, it's supposed to be super dependable, like it works in the harshest conditions. I saw something that showed it working inside a block of ice." His grin widened. "Not that I think you'd need one frozen, unless you're hiking in Alaska or something like that."

"Right."

"And the submersible part I was telling you about? That's also part of the ads, though I guess if one were to get damaged somehow and let water in, they could corrode like you said and cause the light to quit working." He snapped his fingers. "And I bet salt water would have something to do with that too. How did the light get wet?"

"It was dropped in the Atlantic."

His head bobbed. "Yep. Salt water. That'll do it."

"You know a lot about them," Priscilla said, smiling. Actually, he sounded like an infomercial for tactical flashlights, but she kept that to herself. "Do you remember selling one of these recently?"

He shifted to lean his elbow on the counter. "How recently? We sold one a couple of weeks ago to a guy who said he needed something really bright, but I couldn't tell you if it was that particular light. I mean, it looks like the ones we sell, but other than the brand, they're all pretty generic."

Priscilla shook her head. "That's okay."

She swallowed a sudden lump. Deep down, she hoped the person who'd bought the flashlight wasn't Robert. She eased forward and rested her hip against the counter. "Do you remember what the guy looked like?"

He scratched his head. "Normally I would say no. We get too many customers in here for me to remember just one. But this guy sticks out. He had a pretty bad limp. It kinda gave him trouble getting around the store."

She couldn't wait for his description. She had to prompt him. "Was he an older man? Maybe a foot taller than me?"

"An older man?" he repeated, and then shook his head. "I wouldn't say that exactly. Older than me, I guess, but not all that much. Like my dad's age, or maybe a little older."

She blew out a breath. "All right. What else can you remember?"

"He was a tall guy, kinda lanky, you know? Reminded me of a kid I used to play basketball with in high school, except that he didn't really look like an athlete. He wasn't real confident, if you know what I mean. Didn't want to look me in the eyes. I just figured he was distracted and in a hurry."

"He seemed like he was in a hurry?"

"Uh-huh. But I just helped him find what he was looking for." He motioned toward the checkout lanes. "Sandy is the one who actually checked him out. Maybe she could tell you more about him."

"Oh, that would be so helpful," Priscilla said, looking at the cashier with short blonde hair and a stocky build.

"Hold on. I'll get her for you," Joseph said.

His long strides carried him swiftly to the checkout lines. He spoke to Sandy and returned a moment later with her in tow. "Priscilla, this is Sandy. She's our head cashier."

"Pleasure to meet you," Priscilla said. "Thank you so much for talking with me."

"My pleasure," Sandy said, but she looked curious and a little nervous as she twisted the strings of her work apron.

Priscilla picked up the flashlight. "Joseph tells me you sold a flashlight like this one to a man a couple of weeks ago?"

Sandy looked confused by Priscilla's question, but she nodded. "That's right."

"By any chance, it wasn't a young man by the name of Tyler Phillips, was it?" Priscilla asked, playing a hunch.

"Tyler?" Sandy's brows bunched in a troubled knot. "No, I know Tyler. My kids went to school with him. This guy was quite a bit older."

*Older than Tyler but not as old as Robert...*

Still, Joseph had said the flashlight was a popular item, so Tyler could have easily purchased the flashlight somewhere else.

Priscilla pressed on. "Sandy, would you mind if I ask how well you know Tyler?"

Sandy's eyes darkened with concern. She drew back her shoulders and her chin rose. "My husband and I know him very well. Our oldest son is the same age. Tyler used to spend the night at our house pretty frequently when...I mean..." She fumbled to a stop, and her hands fluttered as though she wasn't quite sure what to do with them. Finally, she tucked them into the pockets of her apron. "My husband and I have always had a soft spot for Tyler. I hope he's not in any trouble."

188 | MYSTERIES of MARTHA'S VINEYARD

By the hint of defensiveness in her voice, Priscilla doubted she'd lend an unkind word about Tyler if she thought he was in trouble. Priscilla shook her head. "Oh, no. It's not that at all. It's just, he found my dog the other day, but when I tried to speak to him about it, he acted very strangely. I just wasn't sure why."

"Were you asking him questions?" Sandy asked.

"I did ask him a few," Priscilla admitted. "You see, I have an invisible fence around my yard, and the person who installed it insists that it's working perfectly, which is why I can't understand how my dog got out. Since Tyler was the one who found him, I was just trying to get a little information."

"I see." She looked at Joseph. "Would you give us a minute?"

He nodded. "No problem."

"Oh, but please don't go far," Priscilla urged. "I have a couple more questions I'd like to ask you."

He gave her a thumbs-up and moved to an aisle a few rows over and began stocking shelves.

"Sorry about that," Sandy said, smoothing the hair from her brow. "It's just such a sad story. And I didn't feel right talking about Tyler's past in front of Joseph. I wouldn't even tell you, except that maybe I can explain why his behavior might have appeared odd." She sighed. "It all happened such a long time ago. I've heard he's doing a lot better now, but every once in a while, I think his past still bothers him, especially when he feels like he's being put on the spot."

"Like when I was talking to him at the vet's office?"

Sandy nodded, and her gaze softened to become sympathetic and pleading. "Tyler never did do well with questions, even when he was young. He was always so worried about doing or saying the wrong thing." She leaned in closer and lowered her voice. "You see, Tyler was abused as a kid. He ended up in foster care when he was eleven or twelve, and it made him a little skittish around people he doesn't know. It's really not his fault. He just . . ." She shrugged and lifted her hands. "My husband and I tried to help him. We invited him to church and took him on youth trips, but he was such a lonely kid. It was hard drawing him out of his shell. Unfortunately, I lost track of him after high school, but I'm sure I would know him if I saw him again."

"He didn't keep in touch?"

She shook her head. "I think he wanted to put that part of his life behind him."

"But he didn't move away from the island. Why do you suppose he stayed?"

"His grandmother lives over near Chilmark. I think he pops in to visit her every now and then. Also, I think he just wanted to stay close to where he grew up. It was familiar, after all, even if many of the memories were painful."

"I see. Yes, that would make sense." Priscilla held up the light. "So had you ever seen the guy who bought this before?"

Sandy crossed her arms adamantly. "Not at all. I'd remember him if I had. He looked pretty rough."

Priscilla motioned for Joseph to come back and asked him the same question.

"No, sorry," he said, running his hand through his hair. "I didn't recognize him. He must have been a tourist."

Priscilla bit her lip, thinking. "Okay, that helps me some. What about a name? Did he use a credit or debit card?"

Sandy shook her head. "No. He paid with cash."

Joseph snapped his fingers. "Oh, but he did ask about a hat."

"That's right," Sandy said. "I forgot about that."

Recalling the figure she'd seen fleeing from her cottage, Priscilla stared, wide-eyed. "Do you remember what kind of hat?"

"Just a regular knit hat. It was one of those from the display rack by the door." Sandy looked at Joseph. "I think it was black, right?"

"Yep. We keep hats and gloves handy just because this time of year, people need stuff like that," Joseph explained. "In the summer, we rotate the stock and put in stuff like tumblers and ice chests."

Priscilla's heart beat faster at the mention of the hat. It had to be the same person she'd seen outside the cottage. It was too much of a coincidence otherwise. "Did he buy anything else?"

The two looked at each other, and then Sandy shook her head. "I think that was all." Lines had begun forming at the checkout lanes. One of the other cashiers gave Sandy a wave, and she lifted her hand in response. "Be right there," she called.

"I'm so sorry, I just have one last thing," Priscilla said hopefully. At Sandy's nod, she slid the photos from her purse. "By any chance, the man you saw wouldn't happen to be one of these people, would he?"

Sandy and Joseph studied the photos a moment, and then Joseph pointed to the younger man. "That guy kinda looks like him. Wouldn't you say, Sandy?"

She frowned. "I'm not sure. The guy I sold the flashlight to didn't have a beard."

"No, but look at his eyes," Joseph insisted, angling the photo toward her. "They kinda look like the guy who bought the flashlight."

Sandy squinted for a closer look, then gave a hesitant shrug. "It could be him, I suppose. He sort of looks like him. Maybe without the beard."

They looked expectantly at her as Joseph handed the photos back to Priscilla. "So, who are they—the people in the pictures, I mean?"

"That's what I'm trying to find out," Priscilla said, slipping the photos safely away. She fidgeted, knowing they were hoping for more of an explanation. "Anyway, thank you both so much for your help. I'm sorry I took up so much of your time."

"No problem," Joseph said, and Sandy added a wave as Priscilla turned for the exit.

She climbed into her car and turned on the heater before staring at the photos again. Joseph had said he thought he recognized the younger man without the beard. She placed her thumb over the bottom half of the photo.

The man from the Steamship Authority stared back at her—or at least someone who resembled him. Clark Williams was leaner and wore his hair shorter, but there was a similarity. She tried to imagine Clark with a beard and decided it wasn't that large of a stretch.

Fingers trembling with excitement, she snatched her phone out of her purse and looked up the number for the Steamship Authority. Unfortunately, the woman she had spoken to before—Ethel—wasn't scheduled to work until later that day.

Priscilla left a callback number and then pointed her car toward home. At the last moment, she changed her mind and turned for the Coast Guard station. As she'd hoped, Gerald's SUV was parked in its regular spot. She grabbed the flashlight and headed inside.

Gerald looked pleased to see her, causing a flutter in Priscilla's belly—which of course was silly since he was merely a friend. She cleared her throat and laid the flashlight on his desk.

He looked at the flashlight and then at her. "Let me guess—you found the owner?"

"Possibly." She told him about her visit to the hardware store, complete with Joseph's infomercial regarding the signal strength. "He insisted this flashlight was strong enough to be seen from a couple of nautical miles away. Is that true? Two miles seems so far."

Gerald leaned back in his chair and rubbed his chin thoughtfully. "Absolutely, especially on a clear night. Why? What are you thinking?"

"It occurred to me that when Hannah said she thought something was wrong with the lighthouse, what if what she actually saw was this?" Priscilla tapped the flashlight. "Would that be possible?"

Gerald sat forward and picked up the light. "Possible, yes, especially since my guys said everything is fine with the light-house. I would say it's possible that Hannah saw the lighthouse beam intermittently broken with weaker flashes from a light like this one, and that could explain why she thought something was broken."

Priscilla pressed her palms together tightly. She was certain she'd pinpointed what happened with the light. If only she could be as certain about the photos.

Startled by the ringing of her cell phone, Priscilla glanced at the display screen. Recognizing the number as coming from the Steamship Authority, she excused herself and strode into the hall outside his office to answer.

"Priscilla? This is Ethel from the Steamship Authority."

"Hello, Ethel. Thank you for returning my call."

Quickly, Priscilla explained what she needed while she paced. "The man I'm talking about would have talked to you soon after I left," she finished. "In fact, I almost bumped into him."

"Oh, yes, I remember him," Ethel said. "He was somewhat of a larger man—lengthwise I mean, not breadth." She gave a light-hearted chuckle, then added, "And he seemed a little in a hurry."

"That was the impression I got too. Did he say what he wanted?"

Ethel made a soft tsking sound. "Well, now, that's kind of funny. He asked for the lost and found."

*Bingo!*

Priscilla felt her enthusiasm rising. She quit pacing and stared down at the tiled floor. "He didn't by any chance say what he was looking for, did he?"

"Yes, as a matter of fact, he did. I was going to call you soon to ask if he got in touch with you. He was looking for a suitcase—isn't that amazing? Right after you told me you found one! Anyway, I gave him your name and told him you owned the lighthouse on Misty Harbor. He said he would get a hold of you and see if you'd found his suitcase."

Priscilla sucked in a breath and reached for the sill below a long bank of windows overlooking the water. "Wait, you told him I was there asking about a suitcase?"

"Well...yes. Shouldn't I have?" The humor in her tone fled.

Priscilla forced her breathing to slow. "It's all right, Ethel. I just...do you remember exactly what you said? It's very important."

Ethel hesitated, and worry brought a quiver to her voice. "Well, he asked if anyone had turned in a suitcase, and I told him that someone had just come in asking if anyone had lost a suitcase, and that there must be something in the air. We sort of joked about it and then...oh, dear."

Priscilla's grip on the sill tightened. "What?"

"I...er...I pointed you out when I said he was the second person to ask me about it. I hope that's all right."

"It's fine," Priscilla assured her quietly. That explained why Clark had followed her to the Nautilus Cafe and asked Tobin about her. "Now, I just need to be sure of one last thing."

"Okay." Though she agreed, Ethel did not sound certain.

"Did he happen to mention what was inside the suitcase he lost?"

"No, he didn't. I remember distinctly." Ethel sounded relieved that she hadn't given away any more confidential information. "He left shortly after we spoke."

"Okay. Thank you very much, Ethel. I really appreciate your help."

Priscilla disconnected, but stayed in the hall a while longer as she thought over everything she'd learned.

"Priscilla? Is everything okay?"

Gerald stood in the hall, watching her with his hands shoved into the pockets of his trousers, concern deepening the lines on his face.

She dropped her hand to her side and nodded. "Yes, everything is fine, thank you, Gerald."

As she walked toward him, he pointed to her phone. "That wasn't Rachel, was it? You took off so quickly, I thought something might be wrong."

Priscilla looked around at the stares directed their way—not meddling, just curious and perhaps a bit concerned. "No, it wasn't Rachel. Would you mind if we stepped back into your office?"

"Of course not." He took her elbow, led her inside, and closed the glass door behind them. "What's going on, Priscilla?"

While she explained about the phone call with Ethel, Gerald crossed to a small refrigerator, took out two bottles of water, and carried them back to the desk. He set one next to Priscilla, but instead of circling around to sit behind the desk, he claimed the chair next to her.

Priscilla clasped her hands. "Anyway, I think it may have been Clark who came by my house and kidnapped Jake. After all, that would certainly explain why Jake doesn't like him."

Gerald gave a confused shake of his head. "I don't understand. How do you know Jake doesn't like him?"

"We bumped into him yesterday at Christmas in Edgartown. Jake saw him and really tensed up the closer we got. The fur on his neck rose, and he even growled."

"What did Clark say about Jake's behavior?"

"He claimed it was because he's so nervous around dogs, but Robert said—"

"Who?"

Priscilla laid her finger over her lips. "Oh, dear. I'm afraid I've left out a few important details."

Starting at the beginning, she told Gerald everything she had learned since last they spoke about the suitcase. She also told him about the break-in at her house, though she did this reluctantly. As Gerald listened, he sat back, his hands gripping the arms of his chair.

"I can only think of two reasons why someone who lost a suitcase and knows I found one around the same time wouldn't come to me and ask to see if it's his," Priscilla continued. "One"—she lifted a finger—"whoever owns the suitcase stole the diamonds I found hidden in the secret compartment and was trying to leave the country with them, or two"—she held up another finger—"he was trying to sell them on the black market."

"You forgot three."

Her brows rose. "Oh?"

"The person who owned the suitcase is no longer *able* to look for it."

She shuddered. "You're right. That is another possibility—though I doubt it." She narrowed her eyes slyly. "Someone broke into my house looking for the suitcase, remember? That's not to say that someone else couldn't have known about the suitcase, but then that would tend to lead us back to the first two scenarios."

He nodded. "All right. Which do *you* think it was?"

Priscilla stared at him steadily. "I'm inclined to believe the second option."

"And why is that?"

She tapped the flashlight. "I think whoever owns the suitcase may have been signaling to someone. I think they may have planned to meet but somehow, the owner got separated from the suitcase and it ended up washing up on my beach. Since the diamonds are stolen, he can't report the suitcase missing. But he can't just walk away either, which leaves him trying to locate the suitcase on his own."

Gerald laced his fingers on the desktop. "I have to admit, it's a pretty good theory."

His next words cut the triumphant smile from her lips.

"Just one thing, though. You keep saying 'he.' Why, Priscilla? What else haven't you told me?"

She lowered her gaze. "It's still just a theory, Gerald. I don't like accusing someone without proof."

"But you have a pretty good idea who the suitcase belongs to, don't you?" he demanded.

Hearing the concern that laced his voice, she forced herself to look into his eyes. "I do," she admitted slowly.

"Well?" He leaned toward her, so close she could see the golden flecks in his hazel eyes.

She took a deep breath, knowing once she spoke her suspicion out loud, she couldn't take it back, then pushed the words out. "I think the suitcase belongs to a man I've run into a couple of times in the past few days and who's been asking around town about me. His name is Clark Williams."

## CHAPTER FIFTEEN

Gerald's lips clamped shut, and the muscles along his jaw hardened. Worse, his eyes took on a resolute gleam. Priscilla sucked in a breath. She knew that look. It was the same expression that came over Gary whenever he was worried about her. It also meant he was getting ready to argue his point, or worse yet, working himself up to put his foot down.

"Priscilla, you do realize you need to go to the police, right?" Gerald spoke carefully, his words slow and measured. "If your suspicions about Clark Wiliams are correct, it's not safe for you to keep that suitcase in your house, especially with him running around the island."

"I only *think* it's him," she reminded him. "I still don't have any proof."

"Whoever it is," he insisted, pressing his palm on the desk, "I don't want them snooping around the cottage again, looking for the suitcase, especially with you there all alone."

He opened his mouth to say more, but before he could utter the words, she raised her hand and nodded.

"I couldn't agree more."

He snapped his mouth closed.

"You're absolutely right. It isn't safe for me to keep the diamonds at my house. He already tried coming after them once. I'm pretty sure he'll try again. It's only a matter of time before he stumbles on my hiding place."

She stifled a laugh at the bemused expression on Gerald's face. Obviously, he'd been expecting an argument and didn't know quite what to do now that he hadn't gotten one.

She laid her hands in her lap and sat up straighter in her chair. "I will contact the police…as soon as I have something concrete to tell them. In the meantime," she continued quickly, before he could list the many reasons why she shouldn't delay, "I think it would be best if we got the diamonds out of my house and into someplace safe. Someplace like…" She directed a pointed glance at Gerald's desk, hoping he would catch her meaning.

He gave a slow, disbelieving blink. "You want to bring the diamonds here?"

"It's either that or leave them where they are," she insisted, squaring her jaw. "I promise, it'll only be temporary, just until I talk to Hank Westin to see what he makes of all this. After all, he may tell me there is nothing the police can do besides try to find the owner of the suitcase."

She held her breath, counting the seconds until Gerald agreed. Finally, he gave a slow nod.

"All right. I'll keep the diamonds safe for you, but only if you promise to go to the police the moment you're sure Williams is your guy," he said, rising. "Or if you feel threatened by him in any way. Let the police deal with him. I hate to think about what could happen if you tried to catch him on your own."

Now that the diamonds were out of the way, relief filled Priscilla's chest. She stood with him. "I promise, Gerald. And thank you."

Instead of moving away, he looked down at her, his gaze troubled...and something more. Something tender. His lips parted.

Priscilla swallowed a sudden knot in her throat and backed away a step. "Anyway, it's not like I'm totally alone. I have the best watchdog on Martha's Vineyard." She tried to sound lighthearted, but Gerald refused to budge.

His head lifted, and he crossed his arms and eyed her steadily. "I'm serious, Priscilla. We have no idea the kind of person we're dealing with. A desperate man could go to any lengths to get what he wants. And let's not forget, it may not even be this Clark Williams we're after at all."

A flush that started somewhere in her middle rose up to warm her neck and cheeks. Gerald could be quite impressive when he was so determined and protective. No doubt that was one of the things that made him such a good Coast Guard captain.

She gave a wave intended to let him know she agreed and cool her cheeks at the same time. "You're right, Gerald. I'll be careful."

Satisfied with her answer, he moved to the door and held it open for her. Still, he looked a little hesitant as she reached for her coat and purse. "You know, Chickie can handle things here just fine on his own. Maybe I should go with you to get the diamonds."

Though his concern for her was touching, Priscilla gave an adamant shake of her head. She had been learning to take care of herself since moving to the island. After losing Gary, it was one of the hardest lessons she'd had to grasp, and therefore one of the most valuable. "Thank you, but there's no need for that, Gerald. I'll be back soon."

She left before she could second-guess her decision or wonder about the odd little nudge in her belly that insisted it might be nice to have someone like Gerald around watching over her again.

The trip home to get the diamonds and deliver them to the station didn't take long, which gave her plenty of time when she returned home to eat a hasty late lunch. When she finished, she headed to the bathroom to freshen up and change before meeting Gail in Edgartown.

Despite the chill in the air, the walking tour was nice, with the entire town of Edgartown proudly displaying its Christmas finery. Far better was the fact that it gave Priscilla plenty of time to explain to Gail everything that had happened since she'd seen her last. Plus, the excited hubbub created by the tour guests meant she didn't have to fret about being overheard. Not that she need have worried. People were much too engaged pointing out extravagant light displays and sipping hot chocolate to notice the two of them.

Gail caught the tail end of her fluttering scarf and shoved it deep into her coat. "You're sure it's Clark's suitcase?" she asked, turning sideways to ease around a display of lighted Christmas trees. She bumped an ornament, righted it before it could tumble to the ground, and turned a stern look on Priscilla. "What about Tyler? Jake didn't much care for him either, remember? He started barking the moment he saw him. And Tyler acted so oddly when you started asking him questions. Oh, and don't forget it could have been him we spotted running from the cottage."

A group of carolers dressed in costumes that looked like they'd been pulled from the pages of a Dickens novel chose that exact moment to strike up a lively tune. Priscilla waited until they passed before responding.

"He was acting a bit strange, but I think I know why," she said, and went on to tell Gail what she'd learned of Tyler's past.

"That really is a sad story," Gail said when she finished. She tucked her arm through Priscilla's. "That's why I love events like this one. Part of the money raised goes to help children dealing with similar circumstances." She made a *tsk* sound and looked sidelong at Priscilla. "We were pretty lucky growing up with the families we had, eh?"

"We're still lucky," Priscilla said, giving her cousin's hand a pat. "Do you remember that time when Aunt Marjorie made us all take swimming lessons because I told her I wanted to learn to sail?"

"And we all decided we wanted to learn too because we had images of dashing pirates in our heads." Gail chuckled. "She was certain we'd all drown and it would be her fault because you had come to visit her."

"She could really be tough when she set her mind to something," Priscilla said with a groan.

Gail held up a finger. "But I did learn to swim that summer."

"Me too!" Priscilla laughed. "Say, what are Trudy and Joan doing tonight? Will they be at the Lighting of the Lighthouse?"

"Trudy will. Joan said she wasn't feeling well and decided to stay home. There must be some sort of bug going around."

"Aw, that's too bad."

"She said she came down with it at work. Hopefully it's just a little stomach bug. I sure wouldn't want her to be sick so close to Christmas."

"Hmm." Priscilla eyed a collection of ceramic ornaments dangling from a display in one of the store windows. One was a small glass sparrow with a bit of blue ribbon in its beak. It reminded her instantly of Joan. "Maybe we can find her a little something—" She stopped and stared at the tall figure stepping from a car in a nearby parking lot. "Gail, look."

"What is it?"

She drew Gail to a halt and pointed. "Over there, going into that hotel. It's Clark Williams. He said he was a tourist. That must be where he's staying."

"And?" Gail narrowed her eyes suspiciously. "You don't intend to go in there after him, do you? I thought you said you promised Gerald that you'd let the police handle it."

Priscilla shot another glance at the door and then looked at Gail.

Gail let go of her arm and propped her hands on her hips. "Priscilla Grant, what on earth do you have planned?"

## CHAPTER SIXTEEN

Priscilla grabbed Gail's hand and pulled her toward the hotel. Already, an idea was taking shape, but in order for it to work, they needed to make sure Clark saw them before he headed to his room.

"Whatever you do," she said, ducking around a couple who were intently studying a map of the town, "make sure you act natural. Don't stare at him."

Steps from the entrance, Gail dug in her heels and pulled Priscilla to a stop.

"Don't stare? Priscilla, how am I supposed to do that? As for acting natural..." She jammed her fists onto her hips. "I'm a hygienist. If you want me to act natural, I'm going to have to ask him to open wide and try not to swallow. I am not a detective. Come to think of it, neither are you."

Priscilla glanced at the door and back to Gail. Even now, Clark could be disappearing into an elevator or a hallway. Her desperation rising, she held her hands up and her voice turned pleading. "You're right. We're not the police. Which is why we're not going to do anything silly or dangerous."

Gail's eyes narrowed suspiciously. "We're not?"

"Absolutely not. All we're going to do is drop a few hints and see if Clark will take the bait."

Color rose to Gail's cheeks. "And if he does?"

"We'll call Chief Westin," Priscilla said firmly.

Her assurance seemed to appease Gail somewhat, but there was still a skeptical set to her jaw. "What do I say? How should I act?"

Priscilla could almost feel the precious seconds ticking away. She reached for the door handle and gave a flustered wave. "Just…follow my lead, okay? Let's go."

Behind her, Priscilla could hear Gail muttering protests under her breath—things like "harebrained idea" and "we're going to get ourselves killed."

Warm air whooshed through the door as they went inside, accompanied by merry holiday tunes piped over the hotel sound system. Priscilla scanned the lobby area, fraught with Christmas decorations that made it impossible to see the sides of the room clearly. Spotting the front desk, she began easing her way toward it, all while searching for signs of Clark. She finally spied him a short distance away. He stood in front of the elevators, his head down and a newspaper tucked under his arm.

"There he is," Priscilla whispered. She quickened her pace, then shot a glance over her shoulder at Gail. "I'll do the talking. You just nod your head every now and then like you agree with what I'm saying."

Gail's face puckered as though she'd sucked on a lemon, but she kept pace with Priscilla as they approached the vacant check-in counter. Priscilla rang the bell and laid her arms casually on the cool marble top.

"Here we are, Gail. Let's ask the receptionist if she knows of any guests who might be missing a suitcase."

Though she spoke loudly enough for him to hear, Clark didn't budge. Priscilla frowned. In fact, other than a cursory glance in their direction, he didn't seem interested in them at all.

Gail's gaze darted back and forth between Priscilla and Clark. "Yeah, um, maybe we'll get lucky and find the person who lost it. On your beach. The other day. When you found it."

Priscilla's eyes widened the more Gail talked. Finally, Gail stumbled to a stop.

"What are you doing?" Priscilla whispered, twisting for a glimpse of the elevators.

"I have no idea," Gail whispered back. She matched Priscilla's posture and laid her arms on top of the marble counter. "I told you, I'm not good at this."

Priscilla sighed and turned her attention to Clark. Unfortunately, he'd moved behind a tall artificial Christmas tree. From this angle, she wouldn't be able to see if he got on the elevator.

"Can I help you, ladies?"

Both Priscilla and Gail startled at the voice. The hotel desk clerk eyed them curiously, and when they looked at her, she raised her brows.

"I'm sorry, were you talking to us?" Priscilla said.

The woman, who looked proper and stiff in her pert blue uniform and starched shirt, put on a professional smile and laid her clasped hands on the counter. "Were you wanting to check in?" She pointed to a No Vacancy sign on the desk. "Because unfortunately, we are completely booked for the duration of the festival."

Gail gave Priscilla a nudge with her elbow. Priscilla ignored her, or tried to, which was increasingly hard with Gail glaring at her.

Priscilla dismissed the desk clerk's question with a wave. "No, no, we don't need a room, thank you. We were just wondering if perhaps one of your guests has left any messages with you regarding a missing suitcase."

The desk clerk tilted her head questioningly. "I'm sorry?"

"Forgive me. I should probably introduce myself." Priscilla laid her hand over her chest. "I'm Priscilla Grant. I own the lighthouse over in Misty Harbor." She grasped Gail's shoulder. "This is my cousin, Gail."

"How do you do?" Though the clerk maintained her professionalism, it was obvious by the mingled look of curiosity and impatience that she was wondering what they were doing in her hotel.

Priscilla forced a smile and raised her voice slightly, enough so that Clark could hear from the hallway, if he was still there.

"My dog found a suitcase on the beach outside my cottage the other day, and I've been stopping by several of the local businesses, trying to find the owner."

The confusion cleared from the clerk's face, replaced by a sudden spark of interest. "Oh, really? A suitcase. How strange. Do you have any idea how it got there?"

"No, I don't. There was no identification that I could find, but there were some photos and a few other personal items inside, which is why I'm trying so hard to find out who it belongs to."

"That's very nice of you."

"Well, I wouldn't want a visitor to our island to have their trip ruined." Priscilla paused and tilted her head toward the elevators a smidge. "I don't suppose any of your guests have reported one missing, have they?"

"Not that I'm aware of, but if you'd like to leave a description..."

While the clerk continued to talk, Priscilla tried nonchalantly to inch away from the desk so she could peek around the corner, but it was no use. There was no way she could see Clark from this angle. She met Gail's gaze and indicated the hall with a slight tilt of her head. Gail's eyes widened, and she gave an almost imperceptible shake of *her* head. Priscilla tried again and received the same nervous response. She had opened her mouth to whisper when the sudden appearance of Clark himself snapped it shut again.

He smiled benignly at them both. "Good evening, Mrs. Grant. How nice to see you again. Who's your friend?"

"Uh..." Priscilla glanced over at Gail, who was staring wide-eyed at Clark. She slid her foot over and nudged Gail with her toe. "This is my cousin, Gail Smith."

Clark extended his hand. "Pleasure to meet you, Ms. Smith—or is it missus?"

"It's... either is fine," Gail stammered.

And then, whether because of nerves or because she felt compelled to action, Gail curtsied.

Priscilla watched in delighted dismay. "Um…"

"Can I help you with something, Mr. Williams?" the desk clerk asked.

He smiled and motioned toward Priscilla and Gail. "I'm in no hurry. Please finish helping these ladies."

"Thank you—" Gail began.

Priscilla grabbed her arm before she could finish and gestured Clark forward. "We wouldn't dream of holding you up. Please, go ahead."

She stuck her chin out stubbornly and waited. Clark would either have to admit he'd been eavesdropping or come up with an excuse for remaining in the lobby.

He nodded and stepped forward to lay his newspaper on the counter. "It's silly, really. I was reading the paper and noticed I'm missing a section."

The desk clerk reached for the paper and slid it closer. "Oh, no. I'm so sorry. That does happen sometimes. Which section are you missing?"

"The sports section." Clark shoved his hands into his pockets and stood, rocking on his heels, while he waited for the desk clerk to bring him another paper. His eyes met Priscilla's, and he offered another smile. "So, Mrs. Grant, did I overhear you say something about finding a suitcase?"

Aha! Priscilla wanted to pump her fist in victory but instead chose to smile as though they were chatting about the weather.

"Yes, you did, in fact. I have to say, it's the strangest thing I've ever come upon. It just washed up on my beach out of nowhere."

The clerk returned and handed Clark a folded copy of the paper. "Here you are, Mr. Williams. My apologies again."

"Not a problem," he said as he tucked the paper under his arm. "Thank you so much."

The clerk directed her attention back to Priscilla. "Anything else I can do for you, ladies?"

Priscilla smiled and shook her head. "Nothing, thank you."

"All right." The clerk motioned toward an office to her left. "I'll be right in there. If you need anything, just ring the bell." She pushed the bell toward them and then disappeared.

Clark turned casually toward Priscilla, but the eagerness in his eyes gave him away. He was feeling anything but casual. "So, what kind of suitcase did you find? Was there anything inside?"

Next to her, Gail sucked in an audible breath. Priscilla ignored her and nodded. "Yes, we did find a few interesting things inside, but nothing that would indicate where the suitcase came from or who it belongs to." She gave a flick of her fingers. "I'm headed home to get it now, actually. Since I haven't been able to find the owner on my own, I've decided to go ahead and turn the suitcase over to the police."

"That's probably a good idea," Clark said, his voice calm and noncommittal. "Too bad you couldn't find the owner. I'm sure they're missing it by now."

While he spoke, Priscilla gauged his reaction carefully. Once again, it was his eyes that gave him away. They darted all over the room, showing his obvious anxiety to get away. She kept her eyes calm, so as not to draw his attention to the fact that she had spotted the telltale sign.

He gave a nod to Gail and another to Priscilla. "Well, good luck, ladies, and good day."

"You too," Gail said weakly. As he strode away, she sagged against the counter. "Thank goodness that's over. Can we go now?"

"Not quite." Priscilla inched around the corner just as the elevator doors slid shut. She reached back and grabbed Gail's hand. "C'mon."

"What are we doing?" Gail protested, her dragging feet making a swooshing sound against the carpet. "Priscilla?"

Priscilla hurried toward the elevators. This was a hotel lobby like any other, which meant there had to be a trash can nearby. Finally she spotted one, a tall metal can situated next to a long, low coffee bar. "We're looking for something."

When they reached the trash can, she dropped Gail's hand and motioned toward the front desk. "Keep an eye out for me. If the clerk comes back, warn me."

"What? Why?" Gail's hands fluttered toward her face as Priscilla took the top off the trash can. "Priscilla, what are you doing?" she exclaimed in a harsh whisper. Her feet danced nervously as she craned her neck to see around the elevator toward the front desk. "What are you looking for?"

The trash can was nearly empty, so Priscilla had to bend quite far inside. She groaned. Her hair would smell like coffee and cigarettes for at least a week. "I thought this was a nonsmoking establishment," she said, her voice hollow and echoing inside the trash can. She felt a tug on her coat and nearly bumped her head as she straightened and pulled her prize out with her. "Got it!"

"Dumpster diving? Really?" Gail scowled in irritation and stomped her foot. "What in the world could be so important that you'd go digging through the trash?"

Smiling, Priscilla turned the paper around so Gail could see. "It's today's paper," she said proudly. "The sports section, in fact. He *was* eavesdropping. He overheard us talking about the suitcase, and he needed an excuse to come over to the desk." She tapped the side of the can. "This should be all I need to prove Clark's involvement . . ."

"But?" Gail said.

Priscilla frowned. "Something still bothers me."

Gail let out a heavy sigh and ran her fingers through her hair. "I'm afraid to ask."

Priscilla folded up the paper and shoved it into her coat pocket. "C'mon, Gail. There's something I need you to do."

"Not again. Didn't you learn your lesson the last time you asked me to do something? I mean, I curtsied, for goodness' sake." She rolled her eyes toward the ceiling in disgust.

"That was a little odd," Priscilla said, laughing. "But it was also entertaining." Gail groaned, and Priscilla took her arm. "Don't worry. I promise, this won't be nearly as challenging. All I need you to do is make a couple of phone calls."

"All right. And what are *you* going to do?"

Priscilla smiled slyly. "I'm going to catch a thief."

# CHAPTER SEVENTEEN

Priscilla sat quietly in her living room and tried very hard to ignore the prickling sensation on her arms and the back of her neck. The television was on, the glare from the screen casting flickering shadows on the walls and ceiling, but the volume was low enough so that she—or Jake—could hear if anyone approached. And someone would approach. Any minute now, if her guess was correct.

She blew out a long breath, trying very hard not to let her nervousness show, which was difficult, considering she was shaking in her shoes. Jake lay at her feet, his quiet snores muffled against the antique braided rug on the floor. A commercial for whitening toothpaste cut into the telecast, and Priscilla reminded herself to shift slightly so she didn't look like a mannequin propped up in her aunt Marjorie's favorite wingback chair.

Tuning out the drone of the television, Priscilla clutched the arms of her chair. Twice, she'd had to force her fingers to stop drumming the sides. She wanted to look calm and composed in case Clark peeked through the windows.

She couldn't help it. She strained to see out the darkened windows, half-expecting to see his pale face peering back. The thought sent a shiver up her spine. Sensing her discomfort, Jake lifted his head and stared up at her, his brown nose twitching.

"It's all right, Jake," Priscilla said, smoothing the fur behind his ears. And she dearly hoped it would be, assuming Gail did exactly as instructed.

Once again, her gaze flitted to the clock on the mantel. The minute hand had barely crept forward from the last time she'd checked. Mentally, she counted the minutes since the Lighting of the Lighthouse had been scheduled to begin. Most of the people in the area—tourists and locals alike—would be clustered around the Edgartown lighthouse, and anyone would safely assume that most of the Martha's Vineyard police force would be too busy monitoring that event to take notice of her at all...even if she called for help.

Jake gave a low growl, and the muscles in Priscilla's back and shoulders immediately went taut. Slowly, she reached for the television remote. With one click, silence fell upon the room. Her ears strained to catch whatever sound had sent Jake into high alert. Tension vibrated from his body, and the hair on the back of his neck stood on end.

Barking, Jake jumped to his feet and nearly sent Priscilla into cardiac arrest. She pressed her hand to her chest, certain she could feel the pounding of her heart through the thick fabric of her sweater.

She held the remote out in front of her like a weapon and eased toward the door. Just as she reached it, someone pounded on it, and Priscilla clutched her hand to her heart a second time.

"Hello? Mrs. Grant? It's me, Clark Williams."

Priscilla parted the curtains hanging over the window alongside her front door. Indeed, Clark stood shivering on her doorstep.

He was wearing a heavy overcoat and a dark gray muffler tucked high under his chin, but he wasn't wearing gloves, and his breath billowed up to form a smoky pale wreath around his head.

Drawing a deep breath, Priscilla dropped the curtain back into place, then slid back the deadbolt. She breathed a silent prayer for protection as she forced a smile to her face and opened the door. "Mr. Williams, what a surprise." She motioned past her driveway toward the empty road. "Why aren't you in Edgartown watching the Lighting of the Lighthouse like everyone else?"

"Is that tonight?" His eyebrows rose. "Oh, well, I wasn't really interested in attending anyway."

Priscilla resisted the urge to touch her sweater and reached up to finger her necklace instead. "Really? I guess I just assumed you wouldn't want to miss it, this being your first time to the island and all."

"That's true, but that sort of thing isn't for everyone. Crowds, you know." He shrugged and motioned toward the door. "Mrs. Grant, would you mind if I came in for a minute?"

Behind her, Jake growled. She grabbed him by the collar and pulled him to her side. "Not at all. Please, come in."

Clark stomped his snow-covered boots on the porch, and Priscilla stepped back to allow him to ease past her.

"Thank you," he said, blowing on his hands. "It's quite chilly out there. I bet the people at the lighthouse are going to be huddling together just to keep warm."

Priscilla laughed, but it was strained and a touch too high-pitched. "That just means it's a perfect night for sipping hot chocolate," she said, hoping to sound cheerful and only partially succeeding. She closed the door, then cleared her throat and swept her hand toward the living room. "Would you like to come in and have a seat, Clark?"

He shot a glance at Jake. The dog had stopped growling but kept his eyes firmly fastened on him, his nose and whiskers quivering. Clark gave a wave and then pushed his hands into the pockets of his coat. "Nah, that's all right. Thanks, anyway."

She clasped her hands behind her back to hide their shaking. "Okay, then, what can I do for you?"

Clark's feet shuffled clumsily, and he reached up to unwind the muffler from around his neck. "I really just wanted to stop by and talk with you about that suitcase you said you found."

She did her best to feign surprise. "Oh? Do you know something about it?"

"Possibly. Maybe. It's kinda hard to say without seeing it first. Would...um...would you mind if I took a look at it? I lost one recently in a minor boating accident just up the coast, not far from here. I thought I would stop by on the off chance that it's mine."

"I suppose it could be yours," she said. "But I don't understand. Why didn't you say something back at the hotel? Or report it missing to the police?"

"Oh, that." He grinned sheepishly. "It's so silly. The suitcase really isn't valuable. I didn't report it missing because I didn't think there would be any chance of recovering it." He shrugged and pulled the muffler from around his neck, then wound it around both hands.

*Like a rope.* Priscilla's throat went dry. She tightened her grip on Jake's collar and tried not to watch.

Suddenly Clark's demeanor changed, became demanding in a subtle but menacing way that raised goose bumps on her flesh. He took a step toward her, putting Jake instantly on guard. Her dog stiffened, and the fur rose on the back of his neck.

"Good dog, Jake," she whispered, lifting her chin and staring Clark in the eyes.

He dropped his gaze to Jake and then back up to Priscilla. "I really do have to insist that I see that suitcase."

His meaning was clear. She could either comply or...

She clenched her jaw and motioned toward the kitchen. "I won't try to stop you. It's on the table, just through there."

His gaze drifted in the direction she pointed. Instead of moving, he set his muffler on the hall table, then swept out his hand and inclined his head. "After you."

Her spine stiff, Priscilla walked into the kitchen, flipped on the light, and then crossed to the counter and wrapped her arms tightly around her middle. Whining softly, Jake followed on her heels, but he kept looking back at Clark and then at her, his gaze questioning.

Clark motioned toward the back door. "I don't trust that dog. Put him outside."

"I'm fairly certain he doesn't trust you, either," she replied, bristling. Still, she didn't want Jake to get hurt. She slid her fingers under his collar. "C'mon, Jake."

Clark reached for the knob and pulled the back door open, all the while standing behind it to keep the door between him and Jake while Priscilla coaxed him outside. Once the dog was outside, Clark slammed the door and then strode to the suitcase and threw open the top. He dug frantically a moment, tossing the maps on the floor, followed by the clothes. Finally, he looked up with a glower.

"Where is it?" His hair was tousled and wild. His cheeks were flushed. His gaze had taken on a crazed, glassy sheen.

*He looks stark raving mad*, Priscilla thought. Or desperate. And desperate men were liable to do anything.

From this angle, she couldn't read the clock. Did she dare stall for time, or should she just give him what he was searching for? Slowly, she reached under her sweater, into the waistband of her blue jeans, and pulled out the leather pouch. "Is this what you're looking for?"

Clark's expression changed to one of deep relief. He wiped his forehead and started toward her, his hand outstretched, but Priscilla pulled the pouch away before he could snatch it. He stared at her, his mouth agape.

"What are they?" she demanded, clutching the bag to her chest. "What's in this bag?"

Clark snorted and stuck both hands on his hips. "You mean you've had them all this time and you don't know? Maybe you're not as good a sleuth as you imagine yourself to be." His smile melted into a sneer. "That is why you came by the hotel, isn't it? You wanted me to overhear you talking about the suitcase."

She narrowed her eyes. "You're right. I do have a pretty good idea what these are. What I can't figure out is why you've gone to so much trouble to find them."

"Perhaps I can explain," said another voice from behind them.

Priscilla swung around to see who had come through the back door. In the same moment, Clark leaped toward her and sent her careening toward the wall. She caught herself just before she hit, then whirled, expecting to see Chief Westin or one of the other Tisbury police officers standing in her kitchen. Instead, she sucked in a breath and stared, disbelieving, down the barrel of a gun.

The hand that held it belonged to Robert Peterson.

## CHAPTER EIGHTEEN

Robert, what are you doing here? And what are you d-doing with a gun?" she stammered.

Robert's lips curved in a sly—no, it was more like a sinister— smile. He stuck out his free hand and twitched his index finger. "Give me the bag, Priscilla. And no funny business. I would hate to see you get hurt. I mean that. Truly."

Tremors claimed her limbs. She instinctively tightened her hold on the pouch. Her gaze bounced from him to a startled Clark, who stared at Robert with his mouth hanging slack.

"It was *your* suitcase?" she whispered shakily. "All along, I thought it was Clark who'd lost it, but it was you?"

Robert touched his finger to his temple and smiled. "I'm surprised you didn't figure it out. You almost did for a while there. I was certain the knife would give me away, especially when you asked about my tattoo."

Disappointment, raw and bitter, rose up from her gut. She'd liked Robert and had even felt some sympathy for him. No doubt, it was all part of the story he told to keep people like her from finding him out. "So the things you said about your parents and the reason you joined the Marines, it was all a lie?"

Robert shrugged. "Believe it or not, that part was true. My father was a Marine, and he did meet my mother after being wounded. I signed up because I wanted to be just like him. As for the rest?" His lips thinned, turning the edges white against his tanned skin. "I admit, it all gets a bit hazy."

"So then..." Priscilla turned her gaze to Clark. "If the suitcase was Robert's, but you knew what he was carrying inside... does that mean the two of you were working together this entire time?"

Clark grinned ruefully and rubbed his knuckles against his scalp. "Not exactly."

"In a way, I suppose you could say that was the plan," Robert said. He motioned to Clark with the tip of the gun. "I was supposed to sell the diamonds to my friend here, but when he heard you talking around town about a missing suitcase that mysteriously washed up on your beach, he thought he would cheat me out of my pay and claim the diamonds for himself." His eyes narrowed to slits as he glared at Clark. "Isn't that right, *Clark*?" He gave a low grunt. "Chose the name after your favorite superhero, did you? I should have known better than to try to deal with an amateur like you."

His eyes grew hard as he leveled the gun at Clark's chest.

Clark spread his palms wide in a placating gesture. "I had no idea the suitcase was yours. For all I knew, you drowned the night your boat capsized in the harbor."

Robert's lips thinned, but he let Clark's comment pass and turned to Priscilla. "Mrs. Grant, the diamonds, if you please."

So a boat *had* capsized. Gerald must not have known because no one had reported it, including Robert. The trembling in Priscilla's knees crescendoed so powerfully that she feared they might not hold her up. She retreated a step to steady herself against the counter. "All of this—the disguises, the sneaking around—for what? A few measly dollars?"

"Measly?" Robert tipped his head back and laughed. Priscilla flinched at the harsh, throaty sound. After a moment, he calmed and let the grin slide from his face. "Uncut, those diamonds may not be worth much, but under the hand of a skilled gem cutter?" He pointed the gun at Clark again. "Tell her."

Clark hesitated, and Robert released the safety with a somber click. Priscilla's mouth went dry at the deadly gleam in his eye. She turned a pleading gaze on Clark.

"They'll be worth millions," he muttered reluctantly.

"Millions," Robert repeated, his voice so calm and even he might have been commenting on the weather. "And what did I ask for? A fraction of that amount, just enough to let me live out the rest of my life comfortably." His tone grew steely, his face a hard, cold mask that sent shivers coursing through Priscilla's body. "I deserved at least that much after wasting all those years working for an ungrateful government," he continued. "And what did those years get me? Nothing, that's what!"

Color rose in his face, and veins bulged in his neck. He drew a deep breath, obviously struggling to regain control of his emotions. Priscilla held her breath and prayed even more fervently than she had the night Gary died, when she feared she'd be alone the rest of her life.

*God, please don't let him shoot! Don't let him kill Clark.*

"Not even a pension," Robert said, his voice quieting. Still, something about the deadly calm that came over him made Priscilla's breathing quicken and her heart hammer inside her ribs. He lifted the gun an inch and addressed Clark. "And then you come along and try to cheat me out of my share."

"That's not what happened. I told you, I had no idea—" Clark's words broke off and his face paled as Robert's scowl darkened.

"Don't give me that. *You* chose our rendezvous point. You flashed the signals."

The flashlight! Priscilla suddenly realized her mistake. Although she'd been right that what Hannah had seen that night were signal lights, it wasn't the flashlight from the suitcase that made them. Clark had another flashlight and used it to signal from the cliff to Robert in the boat.

Robert continued speaking to Clark. "You intentionally picked the rocky part of the harbor. You knew I might capsize—in fact you hoped I would. Only I turned out to be a better swimmer than you thought. I made it to shore. And instead of meeting me like you said you would, you waited and watched. Only Priscilla found the suitcase before you could. Before either of us could." He shot a smile her way. "And you never went to the police with your discovery. I really should thank you for that, I suppose."

Priscilla shook her head slowly and inched toward the back door. "Don't thank me yet, Robert. The night's still not over."

"What?" His eyes narrowed to slits. "What are you talking about?"

Silence fell, broken only by the quiet hum of the refrigerator.

"Unbelievable." Clark's voice rent the air like a crack of thunder. His face split into a grin, and then he chuckled, and finally laughed outright.

The flush returned to Robert's face. Sweat dotted his forehead and ran in rivulets down his temples. "What's so funny?" he demanded.

Clark swung toward him, his chest heaving as he fought to regain his breath. "Don't you get it? It's an *act*. She's playing us both, or"—he jerked his thumb to his chest—"at least me. You were a surprise to both of us—isn't that right, Mrs. Grant?"

The gun shook in Robert's clenched hand, but he either didn't notice or didn't care. His voice dropped to just above a whisper. "What are you talking about?"

While his attention was on Clark, Priscilla spun into action. She flung the pouch as hard as she could at Robert's head and then dropped to crouch beneath the kitchen table.

"Now!" she screamed.

The back door crashed open, shattering the glass and sending fragments skittering across the floor to Priscilla's feet. Police streamed in amid shouts of "Freeze!" and "Don't move!"

For several seconds, there was only noise and the chaotic stamping of rushing feet. Priscilla cowered with her arms wrapped protectively over her head until she heard Chief Westin's thundering roar rise above the din.

"Drop your weapon!" he ordered. He leveled his gun at Robert. Several other officers surrounded Clark, who seemed only too happy to surrender himself rather than face Robert.

Priscilla held her breath, watching as Robert slowly lowered his gun to the floor and then straightened and raised his hands. He was immediately seized by the police, who promptly took both him and Clark into custody.

While the officers dragged Clark outside, Chief Westin picked up the leather pouch and then crossed to Priscilla. "Are you all right, Mrs. Grant?"

She grasped the edge of the table and pulled herself to her feet. Trembling took over, and she rubbed her hands over her arms. "I'm fine, Chief, thanks to you and your men."

"Well, without your tip, we never would have come." He grasped her elbow and pulled her gently away from the door. "That was a very brave thing you did."

"I didn't feel brave," Priscilla said, laughing nervously. "I've never been so scared in my life."

"Well, thankfully, it's all over now." Loosening the string, he poured the contents of the pouch into his hand.

Robert's mouth fell open and his eyes took on the rounded look of saucers. "Rocks?" He strained against the officers holding him. "That can't be! Where are my diamonds?"

"Thanks to our friend here, those stones are in safekeeping." Chief Westin smiled and gave a tilt of his head to Priscilla. "Looks like you were right about the diamonds."

"Apparently." She crossed her arms, smiling as her heart rate gradually slowed to normal. "Good thing we substituted those rocks. They came in handy distracting Robert." She grabbed the chief by the arm. "You got the real ones from Gerald?"

He nodded. "I have an officer on the way to meet him right now."

"I don't understand," Robert growled as his hands were cuffed behind his back. "If you knew what they were, why didn't you go to the police? Unless…" Realization dawned on his face, and with it, a rueful grin. "When did you find out what they were worth?"

Priscilla lifted one shoulder. "It wasn't too hard figuring out how much the diamonds were worth. Once I knew for sure what they were, a little investigating on the internet told me everything I needed to know. As for you and Clark?" She smiled sadly. "I knew he had to be involved somehow. What I couldn't figure out was what he was doing with a World War II Marine Raider stiletto. That led me to you. I wasn't sure how you were involved, and I really hoped you weren't. As for tonight?" She shook her head sadly. "I had no idea you would show up here. The plan was just to catch Clark and use his testimony to locate his contact."

He gave a derisive snort. "I should have known you would figure it out."

"For what it's worth, I really hoped I was wrong," Priscilla said. "Why did you do it? Aside from the money, was there another reason you tried to smuggle out the diamonds?"

"Why?" Robert sneered. "Do you really think I needed more of a reason than the money?"

"But you have your pension—" She broke off, remembering what he'd said about not getting one. She shook her head sadly. "You didn't retire, did you? You were forced out. A dishonorable discharge."

Robert's gaze fell, and she knew she'd guessed correctly. And the part about working for the post office? She might never know how much of it had been lies and how much had been truth.

Outside, Jake let out a bark. Priscilla looked at Chief Westin. "I suppose your men can let him go now. Thank you for keeping him safe."

He nodded and crossed to the door to give the order. Seconds later, Jake bounded inside. He scurried straight over to Robert, snarling as he bit into his coat pocket.

"Hey!" Robert yelled, squirming frantically. "Get him off me." He looked on helplessly as Jake tugged back and forth on the cloth until it tore.

"What have you got there, boy?" Chief Westin asked.

While Priscilla grabbed Jake's collar and tugged him away to calm him, Chief Westin checked Robert's pocket. He pulled out a wool cap and held it high. "Reckon this is what he was after?"

Priscilla eyed the hat and nodded. "I saw him wearing it the day he broke into my cottage—after he stole my dog and dropped him off at a vet's office across the island. He bought it at a local hardware store. I'll give you all the information later."

Chief Westin handed the hat to an officer standing nearby. "Bag this for evidence." He pointed toward Robert. "And get him outside."

As he was led away, Robert gave her a grudging tip of his head. Priscilla watched sadly. She really had liked Robert. Deep down, she'd wanted him to be innocent. For a moment, she wondered if he'd lied about his father after all, and then decided it was unlikely, considering the knife he'd carried and the fact that he'd joined the Marines, if only for a brief time.

"Well," Chief Westin said, sliding his gun into his holster, "looks like you were right about this whole diamond thing." He looked puzzled, even a bit chagrined. "Apparently you have a knack for this kind of thing. Are you sure you aren't in the wrong line of work?"

Priscilla smiled and held up her hands in mock surrender. "No thanks, Chief. I've had enough excitement for one night. I'll leave the crime fighting to you and your officers." She arched an eyebrow teasingly. "At least, for now."

He laughed and then motioned toward the broken glass on the floor. "Sorry about your door. I'll see about getting it fixed in the morning. In the meantime, do you have something to cover it with?"

"I'm sure there's an old piece of plywood or something around here somewhere."

The chief nodded and crooked his finger toward one of his men. "See about getting that covered for Mrs. Grant, would you? And get someone else in here to sweep up all this broken glass."

The officer nodded, and Chief Westin turned back to Priscilla.

"Thanks, Chief," she said. "You have the photo of the footprint I sent you?"

He crossed his arms over his chest. "Sure do. I'm sure our experts will be able to get a pretty accurate sense of the person's size and height thanks to the clever angles you shot." He held out his hand. "The wire?"

"Oh." Priscilla had chosen her bulky sweater on purpose to hide the fact that she was wearing a wire and microphone. She reached in and pulled it out. Wrapping it into a small ball, she laid it in his palm. "Here you go, Chief."

He smiled and held it high. "The recording we got from this, plus the footprint and the fingerprints we took from the suitcase, should be all we need to put both of those guys away for a long time."

"So the diamonds were in fact stolen?"

He nodded. "Smuggled out of Brazil about three months ago. Robert was using those photos you found in the suitcase to purchase false identification. He was a master of disguises—a skill he probably learned during his time in the military. I can see why you confused him with Clark. The two of them look so much alike, they could almost be brothers."

"Especially around the eyes," Priscilla said. "Still, I'm a little disappointed that I didn't spot my mistake sooner."

"Don't be. Robert was disguised in every one of those photos, and like I said before, he was a master at it."

"I guess he'd have to be to fool the people in the hardware store into thinking he was so much younger." Priscilla sighed sadly. "He gave up his family, his freedom, even his chance for a new life, all because of greed."

Chief Westin slid the wire into his pocket. "People have given up a lot more, and sometimes for a lot less."

Priscilla frowned. She didn't like it, but the chief was right. She signaled toward her phone. "Do you mind? I better call Gail and let her know that everything is all right. She's probably pacing a hole in her floor as we speak."

He nodded. "Go ahead, but when you're finished, I'll need you to come down to the station so we can get your statement."

"I'll do that, Chief. Thank you."

A short time later, Priscilla stood alone in her quiet cottage. Peace had been restored to the island...for now. Somehow, she had a feeling it might not be permanent. But that was okay.

She picked up a sliver of glass that had been missed by the broom earlier and dropped it into the trash.

As the chief had said, she had a knack for these kinds of things. She was starting to believe him.

## CHAPTER NINETEEN

Priscilla pulled the last ornament from the storage box—a tiny wooden rocking horse bearing the words *Baby's First Christmas*, and hung it on the tree. When Rachel came over later, she'd give it to her so it could be a part of her own Christmas traditions.

With a satisfied sigh, Priscilla stood back to admire her handiwork. Trimming the tree was something she and Gary had always done together. It started when they were a young couple and carried on right up until he died. She touched a glittering piece of tinsel and watched as its colors reflected the twinkling of the lights and the shimmering star on top.

So many memories, some of them bittersweet. Still, there was joy in the season, and she refused to let her grief keep her from participating.

"Thank You, Lord, for giving me a reason to celebrate," she whispered. She took a step back and smiled in satisfaction. "It's a nice tree, don't you agree, Jake?"

Jake lay snoring in front of the fireplace. Warmed by the crackling flames, he didn't even look up.

Priscilla chuckled as she placed the empty ornament box into the plastic tub she'd carried down from the attic. Most of the ornaments were hers. A few had belonged to her aunt Marjorie. The result was a pleasant mix of merry and memories.

The doorbell rang, and Priscilla hurried to hide the tub in the stairwell leading up to the attic for putting away later. Then she turned down the volume on the Christmas music playing on her computer and went to answer the door.

Of course, it was Trudy who arrived first. She looked charmingly festive in her bright red coat and sparkly silver scarf. And she was bearing a gift that looked suspiciously like it came from Candy Lane's Confectionery. There was a round of "Merry Christmas!" and then Priscilla laughed and stepped back to let Trudy and Dan in out of the cold before giving them both a hug.

Trudy gave the bakery box she was holding to Priscilla, and Dan helped her wiggle out of her coat. While he hung their things on the hooks next to the door, she followed Priscilla into the living room. Catching sight of the tree, she froze in her tracks and put her fingers to her mouth. "Oh, Priscilla, the tree looks beautiful."

"Do you think so?" Priscilla set the box on the coffee table and went to stand next to Trudy. "I took some of Aunt Marjorie's decorations down from the attic."

Trudy fingered one of the lace angels Priscilla had found among Marjorie's things. "She would love this. I'm so glad you've found a use for them."

"And look at this." Priscilla led her to the fireplace mantel, where she had placed the nativity she'd found in the attic along with the ornaments.

Trudy let out a small gasp and picked up the tiny figurine of Baby Jesus. "You found it?" She turned rounded eyes to Priscilla. "But how? I thought Marjorie lost this piece years ago."

"She did," Priscilla said, smiling. "I mixed in a few pieces from my own nativity—including that one."

Blinking away tears, Trudy carefully replaced the figurine in the manger, then motioned Dan over to see.

"It's lovely, Priscilla," he said, slipping his arm around Trudy's waist.

The bell rang again, and Priscilla motioned them forward. "There's wassail in the kitchen. Feel free to grab some and then take a look around. I bet you'll spot several more decorations that look familiar."

While they drifted toward the kitchen, Priscilla went to answer the door. Gail and her father, Hugh, waited on the porch, both of them with covered dishes that smelled sweetly of cinnamon and cloves. Right behind them was Joan. She had a platter in her hands, but this one definitely did not look like it had come from a bakery.

Priscilla motioned them all inside. They deposited the dishes in the kitchen and then Priscilla took their coats, smiling as both Gail and Hugh exclaimed over the ornaments on the tree.

"It smells heavenly in here," Joan said. Taking another deep whiff, she said, "Is that hummingbird cake I smell?"

"Did someone say hummingbird?" Hugh asked, his countenance brightening.

"Now, Pop, you know you have to wait until after dinner," Gail scolded gently. She helped her father into a chair and then straightened and rubbed her hands together. "All right, what do you need us to do? Is the table ready?"

"Actually, the table is all set. I have the turkey warming in the oven along with the rolls, and everything else is waiting in serving dishes. All we need now—"

Once again the doorbell rang, and Priscilla laughed as she went to answer.

"Look who I found hanging out on your porch," Rachel said. She dropped her luggage on the floor and pulled Gerald forward. "And it looks like he comes bearing gifts."

In his arms was the largest potted plant Priscilla had ever seen. Gerald smiled sheepishly at her over the top of it. "Hope you like poinsettias."

"I love them." Priscilla motioned him and Rachel inside. "It'll look perfect next to the fireplace."

There was another round of "hello" and "Merry Christmas" from all, and then, while Rachel was enveloped by a swarm of affectionate cousins, Priscilla followed Gerald to the fireplace.

He pointed toward the hearth. "This spot okay?"

"It's perfect." She bent and removed a fluffy stuffed snowman so he could set the plant down, then snuggled the snowman alongside it.

"Nice," Gerald said, smiling as they straightened. He shot a quick glance around the living room. "The cottage looks very festive."

"Thank you. I still have a few lights to hang outside, but I thought I would tackle those after dinner."

"You're not planning on climbing onto the roof, I hope?" he said, his eyebrows raised in alarm.

She laughed and patted his arm. "Don't worry. I've had my fill of danger for this year without taking any chances on a ladder. I'm just going to string a few lights along the railing and around the bushes. Hopefully, Jake will leave them alone."

Gradually, he let his eyebrows fall to their normal place. "Well, I'm glad to hear that." He motioned toward the kitchen. "You were able to get the door fixed?"

"Oh, yes. Actually, I went ahead and replaced it with a new one. Beau Ortmann came over and took care of it for me. It didn't take him any time at all, and I got a much sturdier door out of the deal. This one has a heavy-duty deadbolt on it. Beau assures me it would take a bulldozer to knock it down."

Gerald nodded. "That's good."

Sensing there was more he wanted to say, Priscilla met his gaze. "We haven't had a chance to talk much since Clark and Robert were arrested. I've been meaning to stop by the station and thank you for your part in keeping the diamonds safe until the men could be apprehended."

He shrugged and rested one arm on the mantel. "It was nothing. I'm just glad you're okay. When I heard that Robert was apprehended with a gun . . ." He swallowed hard and jammed his hands into his pockets. "Anyway, I'm glad it's all over and everyone is safe. I'm glad . . . you're safe."

Why he felt compelled to add the last part, she couldn't guess. She dropped her gaze. Or maybe she could guess and just didn't want to in case she was wrong. Or in case she wasn't.

Suddenly, Priscilla became aware that she and Gerald had become the focus of some very interested attention. She pasted a bright smile to her lips and lifted her chin. "Would anyone else like some wassail?"

There were several nods of agreement, and Priscilla looked at Gerald. "You must try a cup, Gerald. It's an old family recipe."

"I'd love some," he said, following her and the others to the kitchen.

Once everyone had a cup, Priscilla raised hers high, savoring the smell of citrus and cinnamon and the happy smiles on the faces of all the people she loved.

"Thank you all so much for coming," she began. "As you know, this is the second Christmas for Rachel and me that's different from others we have known." She shared a long glance with her daughter, saddened by the sorrow she saw glimmering in her eyes and determined to do something about it. Her chin rose. "Still, I'm so happy to be here with you all. I can't imagine spending it anywhere else. Will you join me in a toast?"

Glasses lifted to join hers. She smiled.

"To Christmas," she said, "and to time spent with those we love. May we never take either one for granted."

The words "To Christmas!" resounded in her small kitchen. Even Jake added a happy bark as china clinked against china.

238 | MYSTERIES *of* MARTHA'S VINEYARD

Watching it all unfold, Priscilla couldn't help but feel as though her heart was overflowing. It had been a long time coming, but she was starting to find her way—starting to feel as though God *still* had a plan and a purpose for her life, and that she would enjoy every moment of discovery along the way.

Across the room, her gaze locked with Gerald's.

Here too was an unexpected surprise, one she could not have planned for but would not shy away from. When the time was right.

She took another sip of her wassail. For now, she would enjoy the warmth and fellowship of good friends and leave the future to her Father. Only He could see what tomorrow would bring.

For her . . . it was all a mystery.

# AUTHOR LETTER

Dear Reader,

I have always loved to read. Ever since I was a little girl, the people I met and the places I visited in books were as vivid and real to me as those I experienced day to day. That's why I'm so thrilled to be writing stories set on Martha's Vineyard. Though I've never visited there in person, I was able to walk the streets along with Priscilla and savor the sights and sounds unique to this very special place. Now that I've written a book set on the island, my husband has promised that we will see it in person . . . possibly next summer! I can't wait to smell the salty sea air and walk the quaint streets. Stay tuned. I promise to share pictures and recipes and not-to-be-missed locations. I'll call it Elizabeth's Entrance to Adventure. I hope you'll join me there.

Enjoy!

Sincerely,
Elizabeth Ludwig

## ABOUT THE AUTHOR

Elizabeth Ludwig is an award-winning author whose work has been featured on Novel Rocket, in *More to Life* magazine, and in *Christian Fiction Online Magazine*. Her first novel, *Where the Truth Lies* (co-authored with Janelle Mowery), earned her the 2008 IWA Writer of the Year Award. This book was followed in 2009 by "I'll be Home for Christmas," part of the Christmas anthology collection *Christmas Homecoming*.

In 2011, her second mystery, *Died in the Wool* (co-authored with Janelle Mowery) was nominated for a Carol Award. In 2012, books one and two of the Edge of Freedom series released from Bethany House Publishers—*No Safe Harbor* and *Dark Road Home*—earned 4 stars from *RT Book Reviews*. Book three in the series, *Tide and Tempest*, received top honors with 4½ stars and was recently named a finalist for the Gayle Wilson Award of Excellence. Elizabeth was also named a finalist in the 2015 Selah Awards for her novella "One Holy Night," part of the best-selling anthology collection *Christmas Comes to Bethlehem, Maine*. Her latest releases include *Home Sweet Sugarcreek* and *A Tempting Taste of Mystery*, part of the Sugarcreek Amish Mysteries series from Guideposts.

Elizabeth is an accomplished speaker and teacher, often attending conferences and seminars, where she lectures on editing for fiction writers, crafting effective novel proposals, and conducting successful editor/agent interviews. Along with her husband and children, she makes her home in the great state of Texas. To learn more, check out ElizabethLudwig.com or visit her on Facebook.

## AN ARMCHAIR TOUR OF
## MARTHA'S VINEYARD

Every year for the past thirty-six years, the residents of Edgartown, Massachusetts, have hosted an annual weekend celebration called Christmas in Edgartown. Not only is this event fun, it helps raise funds for island-wide charities and nonprofit organizations. Among the many things to do and see are an annual Teddy Bear Suite and Christmas Parade, plus a Bah Humbug Walking Tour that is sure to delight. There are even classes for things like wreath making! And what celebration would be complete without food? There are plenty of holiday treats in Edgartown. Wine and cheese tastings, Christmas cookie and chowder contests, cider, and sweets make this a tempting taste of holiday cheer. Finally, there's plenty of shopping to help you finish off your Christmas list. It's a weekend filled with music and fun, one that is sure to become a favorite family vacation for all ages.

## SOMETHING DELICIOUS FROM OUR SEASIDE FRIENDS

### *Christmas Wassail*

**Ingredients:**

2 quarts apple cider

1½ cups orange juice

¼ cup pineapple juice

1 tablespoon brown sugar

½ teaspoon lemon juice

2 cinnamon sticks (3 inches)

Dash ground cinnamon

Dash ground cloves

**Directions**

Combine all the ingredients in a large saucepan. Bring to a boil. Reduce heat, then cover and simmer for 20–30 minutes. Discard cinnamon sticks. Serve hot in mugs.

Yield: 10–12 servings (2½ quarts).

Read on for a sneak peek of another exciting book
in the series Mysteries of Martha's Vineyard!

## A Port in the Storm
by Elizabeth Penney

Martha's Vineyard in the winter. Piles of warm covers on the bed, curtains pulled tightly shut against the cold, and a dog with cabin fever.

At barely seven a.m., according to the digital clock, Jake jumped on the bed and stuck his chilly wet nose right in his owner's ear. Priscilla Latham Grant pushed him away with a groan. "Give me a few more minutes, okay, Jakey? It's too early for you to go out."

In answer, he plopped down on her legs and curled up with a sigh. She reached out a hand to fondle his silky ears, thinking once again what a blessing her adopted dog had been. Especially during this first winter on an island in the Atlantic, far from the Kansas farm that had been her home. For more than three decades, she and her husband Gary had worked together raising wheat, corn, and soybeans, an endeavor that ended with his untimely death less than a year ago.

The inheritance of a lighthouse and cottage from her aunt Marjorie Latham had given Priscilla an opportunity for a new life, one she embraced heartily. Her daughter Rachel, thirty-two and living in Kansas City, hadn't been so sure about her mother's decision. But Priscilla had found peace in it—until these short, dark days had set in, filled with relentless storms battering the island, one after another. Friends and neighbors hunkered down, reluctant to go out in the inclement weather, and Priscilla found herself alone—and lonely.

"Enough of that," she muttered to herself. Indulging in self-pity wasn't healthy in a faith-filled life, and certainly not a godly pursuit. Restless and annoyed at herself, she nudged the dog aside gently and slid from under the covers. After a cup of hot coffee and a hearty breakfast, she'd work on her plans for the small museum she was planning to open by summer. A local company had added the lighthouse to their tour itinerary, and Priscilla wanted to create an exhibit of family history for visitors to enjoy.

Priscilla thrust her feet into fleece-lined slippers—a necessity with the icy wooden floors—and slipped on her fluffy robe. Next she shuffled to the window and pulled the curtains open. Monitoring the weather was a time-honored tradition for island residents, as it had been on the farm. Whether derived from land or sea, family livelihoods depended upon reading the signs correctly.

Instead of the expected gray daylight, blinding sunlight streamed in, making Priscilla blink. Joy and gratitude flooded her heart, sending her spirit soaring. *A sunny day at last.* Once her vision cleared, she drank in the view. Sparkling blue water frosted with tiny whitecaps lay beyond the rocky shore, which was blanketed with a pristine layer of snow. Nestled next to the cottage, the lighthouse stood proud and stalwart, a beacon of safety for the past one hundred years.

What a beautiful place to live, even in the dead of winter.

Jake had jumped off the bed and was waiting at her heels. She bent and ruffled his furry head. "Come on, boy, I'm taking you for a walk." In response, he began to leap and cavort about the room. She laughed. "You know that word, don't you?"

First she washed up and put on long johns and a turtleneck under wool pants and a sweater. Warm layering was a must during a bitter New England winter. Then she and Jake went to the kitchen, where she fed him and made a pot of coffee. While it brewed, she threw on her outdoor gear—a down parka, boots, and hat. After filling an insulated travel mug with steaming java, she pulled on mittens and grabbed Jake's leash. "Come on, boy. Let's go." He didn't need to be told twice.

The phone was ringing when Priscilla stepped back inside the cottage a short while later, her cheeks scoured by fresh air and Jake panting with happy exhaustion. She unclipped Jake and shrugged off her coat, then hurried to answer.

Joan Abernathy was on the line. "Good morning, Priscilla. Did you notice that strange yellow orb in the sky?"

Priscilla laughed. "I sure did. I needed to wear sunglasses against the glare." Getting to know Joan, Gail, and Trudy, her Latham cousins, had been one of the best parts of moving to the island. All three were very different in personality and temperament, and while she loved each equally, Priscilla was closest to quiet, practical Joan.

"Want to meet me at the bakery for breakfast? I haven't been able to get there for days." Joan's droll tone expressed what she thought of that state of affairs. Candy Lane Confectionery was one of the women's favorite haunts.

"I'd love to," Priscilla said. "Great timing, by the way. I was just about to make something to eat."

After making sure Jake was all set with food and water, Priscilla put on her coat again and set off for the village in her SUV, which had lovely heated seats. The icy roads were melting, puddles forming on the road, but tall snow banks still loomed on each side of the winding lane, a reminder of the storms they'd endured.

Slowing for a corner, Priscilla caught a glimpse of her neighbor's historic Cape Cod house through the leafless trees. She admired the way the cozy home nestled between ancient maples, smoke drifting from the chimney in a lazy stream. It was a picture-postcard example of a classic New England structure, like many beautiful homes on the island.

She really ought to go see Rebekah Alden, the elderly woman who lived there. They'd met briefly last summer when Rebekah was puttering around in her flower garden. Priscilla had the impression she was isolated, almost a shut-in. That situation must be so much worse in the winter, when it was unsafe for older folks to walk outside in case they slipped on the ice.

Making a mental resolution to go over soon, perhaps with some homemade baked goods, Priscilla turned her attention to the next tricky corner. Snowbanks not only impeded visibility, they reduced the width of the road to a narrow track.

Down in the village, she easily found a parking space on Beach Road near the bakery, one of the advantages of the off-season. In the summer, it was almost impossible at times to drive through town, let alone park.

Several of the gift stores and emporiums flanking the bakery were closed until spring, but a few had brave Open flags hanging outside their doors. Thankfully the bakery was open year-round. What would she and her cousins do without their frequent fix of Candy's treats?

Priscilla pushed the door open with a jingle of bells, entering the steamy warmth scented with vanilla, coffee, and cinnamon. Pulling off her hat and mittens, she glanced around and spotted petite, dark-haired Joan at one of the dozen small tables in the space. Every other table was filled with patrons chatting, reading the newspaper, or tapping away on laptops.

"It's been crazy in here," Joan said when Priscilla reached the table. "I was lucky to get a table. Everyone seems to have had the same idea."

"We all have cabin fever, I guess." Priscilla stuffed her hat and mittens in her coat sleeves and hung the garment on the back of the chair. She peered at Joan's plate. "What did you get?"

Joan displayed the pastry with a flourish. "A cream puff. They're not just for dessert anymore. Seriously, I thought I deserved it after being snowed in for a week."

Priscilla laughed. "On that note, I think I'll go for some of Candy's hummingbird cake, if she has any. Be right back."

A young woman with cropped brunette locks and elflike features was loading the cases with fresh cookies. She gave Priscilla a brilliant smile that wrinkled a pert, freckled nose. "Good morning. Can I help you?"

"You must be new," Priscilla said. "I haven't seen you here before."

"I just started this week, as a baker and general gal Friday." The young woman set down the tray and smoothed her apron. "I'm Harper Jenson."

"And I'm Priscilla Grant, a devoted customer of this bakery. You'll be seeing a lot of me and my cousins." She nodded at Joan. "Joan is one of them."

"Good to know. What can I get you?" Harper stood poised to take the order.

Priscilla scanned the case. Good, they had hummingbird cake today, made Candy's way with cranberries and cream cheese. "A slice of Tisbury Tizzy and a coffee."

"Great choice." The cheerful Harper beamed with satisfaction as she slid the case open. "That cake is fabulous."

"It sure is. I love everything here." Priscilla's gaze roamed over the muffins, crème horns, cookies, and other treats made on the premises.

She was getting ready to carry her breakfast to the table when Candy Lane, owner of the bakery, emerged from the kitchen, walking with her head down. In her midthirties, Candy was usually an irrepressible bundle of energy. Today it was as if her internal light had dimmed. Even her hair appeared lank and tired. She glanced up and noticed Priscilla. "How are you, Priscilla? Nice day, isn't it?" Her tone belied the cheerful words.

"It certainly is, for a change." Priscilla hesitated, then inquired, "Is everything all right, Candy? You don't seem like your usual self."

Candy ran a hand through her hair, disarranging it. "Is it that obvious?" She glanced around. Harper had darted back into the kitchen, and no customers were standing nearby. "It's been a tough winter," she said in a low voice. "With the bad weather, we're way down in sales. And I've had one unexpected expense after another."

Priscilla's heart squeezed in sympathy. She remembered the anxious times when the weather hadn't cooperated on the farm and they'd lost crops. Or when equipment broke down, always at the worst possible time, it seemed. But God had always provided, sometimes in a miraculous way, if not the way she always expected. "I'll say a prayer for you," she said.

"I appreciate that, Priscilla." Candy gave her a wan smile. "Enjoy your breakfast."

"I will." As Priscilla turned, she spotted a flyer taped to the counter. *Share a Little Love*, it read, with a picture of two intertwined hearts. The flyer gave details on a dinner and dance at the high school on Valentine's Day.

Candy noticed her reading the flyer. "You should come to this. It's a great event that benefits both the homeless shelter and the animal shelter. Everyone in town goes." She gave Priscilla a sly smile. "You can bring a date or not, up to you."

Priscilla felt heat flood her cheeks. Since moving to the island, she'd met a certain Coast Guard captain, Gerald O'Bannon, and they'd become friends. Others kept hinting that she should take the next step and officially start dating, but she wasn't ready. How could she be? Her husband had died just over a year before. And besides, there was no real indication that Gerald thought of her as more than a friend.

*But if he did*, a little voice whispered. *What then?*

Priscilla shrugged off those unsettling thoughts. "I'll think about it. Going, that is." Her cheeks flamed even hotter.

"Go eat." Candy made a shooing motion. "I'll send Harper over with coffee refills in a while."

"Thanks, Candy." Priscilla carried her plate and mug to the table where Joan waited. She settled herself then asked, "Do you attend Share a Little Love?"

Joan, cradling her mug in two hands, nodded. "Wouldn't miss it. Every year the event benefits a different organization. This year it's going to help your church." Faith Fellowship ran a homeless shelter from October to May each year.

"And the shelter, which helps dogs like Jake." Priscilla shared Jake's comical reaction to the snow, how he'd dug his nose in and then flung the fluffy flakes off in surprise.

Joan listened, a wistful expression on her face. "You're making me want another dog." She'd lost her dog, Champ, the previous year.

"I heartily recommend it." Priscilla drained her coffee and with impeccable timing, Harper came around the counter holding a pot. Priscilla waved her mug with a smile.

Harper bustled over. "How is everything?"

"Scrumptious as always," Joan said. "You're new, aren't you?"

"This is Harper Jenson," Priscilla said. "This is my cousin, Joan Abernathy."

The two exchanged greetings. "What brings you to Martha's Vineyard?" Joan asked the young woman.

Still holding the coffeepot, Harper cocked one hip to stand more comfortably. "I'm searching for my family."

## A NOTE FROM THE EDITORS

We hope you enjoyed Mysteries of Martha's Vineyard, published by the Books and Inspirational Media Division of Guideposts, a nonprofit organization that touches millions of lives every day through products and services that inspire, encourage, help you grow in your faith, and celebrate God's love.

Thank you for making a difference with your purchase of this book, which helps fund our many outreach programs to military personnel, prisons, hospitals, nursing homes, and educational institutions.

We also create many useful and uplifting online resources. Visit Guideposts.org to read true stories of hope and inspiration, access OurPrayer network, sign up for free newsletters, download free e-books, join our Facebook community, and follow our stimulating blogs.

To learn about other Guideposts publications, including the best-selling devotional *Daily Guideposts*, go to Guideposts.org/Shop, call (800) 932-2145, or write to Guideposts, PO Box 5815, Harlan, Iowa 51593.

# Sign up for the
# Guideposts Fiction Newsletter
## *and stay up-to-date on the books you love!*

You'll get sneak peeks of new releases, recommendations from other Guideposts readers, and special offers just for you . . .

## *and it's FREE!*

## Just go to Guideposts.org/Newsletters today to sign up.

# Guideposts®

**Visit Guideposts.org/Shop
or call (800) 932-2145**

# Find more inspiring fiction in these best-loved Guideposts series!

## Mysteries of Martha's Vineyard

Come to the shores of this quaint and historic island and dig into a cozy mystery. When a recent widow inherits a lighthouse just off the coast of Massachusetts, she finds exciting adventures, new friends, and renewed hope.

## Tearoom Mysteries

Mix one stately Victorian home, a charming lakeside town in Maine, and two adventurous cousins with a passion for tea and hospitality. Add a large scoop of intriguing mystery and sprinkle generously with faith, family, and friends, and you have the recipe for Tearoom Mysteries.

## Sugarcreek Amish Mysteries

Be intrigued by the suspense and joyful "aha!" moments in these delightful stories. Each book in the series brings together two women of vastly different backgrounds and traditions, who realize there's much more to the "simple life" than meets the eye.

## Mysteries of Silver Peak

Escape to the historic mining town of Silver Peak, Colorado, and discover how one woman's love of antiques helps her solve mysteries buried deep in the town's checkered past.

## Patchwork Mysteries

Discover that life's little mysteries often have a common thread in a series where every novel contains an intriguing whodunit centered around a quilt located in a beautiful New England town.

**To learn more about these books,
visit Guideposts.org/Shop**